Silas' Trail

D.W. Lewis

Lazy K Series
Book 1

ISBN:9781972803097
Renaissance Hands Books
2nd Edition
© 2025 David Lewis

Dedicated to my Pa, William Lewis who
introduced me to Westerns.

Chapter 1

Silas Trent was still hurting as he sat astride the horse, a paint with boots, and looked at his worst enemy who was talking. Henry Locke was distracting him by talking, he could shoot him now. Silas drew his gun, staring down the sight at Jack Thompson. He could see the arrogant look on his face as he dared to suggest he was the rightful owner of the Lazy K. Silas was the rightful owner; he could shoot him right now. He watched Thompson reach for his gun.
Shoot!

Why couldn't he shoot? He should shoot. He was here to avenge his father by killing this man. Thompson drew his gun and fired at Henry Locke, the man that helped him hunt Thompson.
Shoot!

Thompson almost fell out of his saddle; his side was bleeding. Silas wondered if he had fired his gun. No. Locke had fired but hadn't killed him. Now was his chance. Silas heard the shot and watched Thompson's head whip back as Locke shot him between the eyes. Out of the corner of his eyes, Silas saw a blur. He turned and fired. It was easier when he didn't think. He saw a man slump and fall off his horse. He had killed a man. He looked over at Locke, the man who had been about to shoot the man that avenged his father's death, surely, he had done the right thing.

The world started spinning. Everything was a blur. He could see his dead father lying on the ground. He could see Matt bleeding out onto the parched soil. Spinning again, brown and green, spinning. He saw his mother, weeping, holding Matt's hand. But no. It wasn't his mother; it was the mother of

the man lying dead. The mother of the man he killed.
Weeping.

Silas jumped up, it was a nightmare. He looked around the campfire at his companions all sleeping soundly on the ground. The night air was cold, so Silas laid back down and wrapped himself in his blanket. The nightmare had become a regular thing for him. He lay there thinking about all the events that lead to him killing Tom Lassiter. Silas had been after Lassiter's boss, Jack Thompson, a cattle thief who had killed his father. Silas had teamed up with the Locke family up in Colorado to find Thompson and his father's cattle, now his cattle. They had also sent their two sons Cody and Jesse to help him drive the cattle back to his home in Arizona.

They were over a week into the drive home and were camped out in a valley between two ragged peaks. Silas could just make out the outline of them in the night sky. While he personally loved the wider spaces where he grew up, he had to admit the mountains of Colorado were a beautiful place to visit. Silas heard one of his partners moving around, he looked over to see Tobias Kent, one of the men sent with him to help drive the cattle. He could tell that Tobias was looking at him in the dark and slowly moved over in his direction.

"You alright kid?" Tobias whispered once he got close enough. Even though Silas was technically the owner of the drive, all the men were being paid by the Locke family. At fifteen years old, Silas was the youngest in the group. Everyone treated him like an equal most of the time, he worked as hard as everyone, but at camp he still became "kid." It didn't really bother him, since it was a term of fondness and not making fun.

"Bad dream." said Silas.

"Been there" Tobias sighed, "I try to think of something nice."

"Like what?" Silas asked.

"Me? I think of a dancing girl in the saloon back at Victor. Her legs make a man quiver." Tobias looked over at Silas and grinned, "mebbe you're still a bit young for that." Tobias inched back to his bedroll and looked up into the sky, his hands behind his head. Silas was sure he was grinning up at the sky thinking about those legs. Silas rolled onto his side and thought his own good thoughts. Back on the Locke ranch there was a girl, Emily. She was the most beautiful girl he has ever seen; she had blonde hair that looked like spun gold and a smile that made him feel warm inside. As he was thinking thoughts about her, he drifted back off to sleep.

The next morning as they were breaking camp, Cody came over to Silas. He put a hand on the younger man's shoulder and smiled. Cody was over a foot taller than Silas' four foot ten and had dark hair. Silas had long blond hair himself, he didn't much like anyone touching it, so going to the barber wasn't a priority.

"Once we get over the last range, we should be crossing into New Mexico," Cody said, "maybe take us about two days unless something goes wrong."

James Smith, the other man sent along to help, looked up at Cody quickly. "Don't tempt fate," he said with a scowl. Cody laughed and turned to James, "I don't believe in that nonsense," he said. James glared at him but said nothing. Silas could hear him muttering to himself as he rolled up his bedroll and started to get his gear onto his horse.

Silas packed his own gear onto his horse, a paint that Emily had lovingly named Boots. This horse was on loan until he made it out of the mountains, and he could start riding his pony again. He felt sorry for his pony, being used as a pack horse, but it was too uncertain on these rocky slopes to be trusted with a rider.

The men all started the task of getting the cattle moving down the slopes. It was tedious work for the most part, making sure the cows stayed on the trail and didn't wander off. Even though a winter chill was starting to fill the air, it wasn't long before Silas had shrugged his long coat off his shoulders. The men moved amongst the herd prodding on stragglers and making sure none of the cows strayed. While it was a team task, each man was left to their own thoughts. Silas daydreamed about Emily most of the time, some of his thoughts were probably best to keep from her brothers who were riding nearby. Sometimes, though, he thought about his Ma.

Silas had been there when his father and brother were murdered, he had caught a bullet in his side in the fight. His memory of how he got back home was a little vague. He remembers someone finding him and putting him on a horse, but the particulars weren't there. His Ma said it was Jedediah Boone, a rancher who lived close to them, that saved him. After recovering from his wounds, Silas had decided to go after the man that killed his father. His Ma didn't like that idea and told him not to go. After a few weeks of struggling with constant visions of revenge, Silas decided he absolutely had to get his revenge and sneaked out of the house one night when everyone was asleep.

He wasn't sure what his Ma would say when he returned. Mrs. Locke had written a letter to let her know he was ok, but that was a while back. He knew she was probably worried about him, but it was also good to bring back the herd that had been stolen. It wasn't much, a few hundred head, but Silas was confident he could manage them and help him, and his Ma survive.

They came up to a narrow pass between two steep slopes and directed the lead cows toward it, knowing the rest would follow easily. Tobias was in the lead, and it wasn't long before Silas couldn't see him as the pass took a turn downhill. Jesse was a way ahead of him as they had the cows moving in twos and threes through the pass. Cody was behind, with James riding drag at the rear to encourage stragglers.

Suddenly Cody swore and yelled out "rockslide!" Silas looked up and saw rocks tumbling down the slope to the left. Some smaller rocks flew through the air and hit a couple of the cows ahead of Silas, they cried out in pain. This started to make the other cows nervous. While they needed to move fast, they also needed to keep them from stampeding. Silas urged Boots on ahead and tried to get the cattle around him to pick up the pace.

Some of the younger cows were trying to turn and get away from the danger while the older ones seemed to trust the cowboy's urging. More rocks fell and Silas saw a large boulder hit one heifer on head. He heard a sickening crack as her skull caved; she slumped to the side and was caught up in the rush of bodies for a second before being sucked underfoot and was trampled. Silas tried to keep one eye on the herd and one on the rocks.

He heard Jesse grunt as a smaller rock hit him. "You hurt?" Cody yelled across at him.

"Hit my arm," yells Jesse, "I'm not sure it isn't broken." Cody swore again as he pushed closer to his brother. Jesse waved him off, "just get through this, I'll be ok."

Silas breathed a sigh of relief as he saw an opening ahead, letting out into a wide space. As he urged the cattle through it he looked back. From the looks of it the rockslide had slowed down. As the last of the herd came down into the valley floor they had entered. James brought the last of them into the valley and the men all worked to stop the cattle moving. There was a spring over to the right side of the valley feeding into a pond, and the cows all wandered over to get something to drink.

As soon as things looked settled Cody rushed over to his brother. Jesse was cradling his left arm in his right and looked a little pale. Cody got off his horse and helped Jesse down and took a close look at the arm. It was bruised and starting to swell.

"How does it feel?" Cody asked.

"I'm pretty sure it's broken," Jesse said through gritted teeth. Tobias rode over to them and got off his horse. Tobias went to his saddlebag and took a kerchief out and looked around for two straight branches about the same length. He walked back over to Jesse and looked at his arm.

"Looks broke to me," he told Jesse, "I kin splint it, but that'll hurt. Mebbe best to get a swig of whiskey." James rode over and pulled a whiskey bottle out of his saddle bag. Cody gave him a look; the Locke family had a policy against drinking on a drive.

James saw the look and shrugged, "good thing I brought it," he said. He handed it down to Tobias who tipped the bottle up to Jesse's lips. Jesse took a swallow and coughed little. Tobias straightened Jesse's arm and the look on Jesse's face showed the Whiskey wasn't doing much to help. Tobias lined up the branches and expertly tied them on with the kerchief from his bag and the one he had tied around his neck.

The sun was still high in the sky, but the men all decided it was time to set up camp to let Jesse rest. Cody got Jesse's bedroll off his horse and got him situated, sitting against a fallen tree. Silas staked the horses and spent some time getting their saddles off and rubbing them down. The horses seemed to appreciate an early quitting time, chomping on the long grass in the valley. James rode over to the herd to keep watch over them and keep them from wandering off. It was a bit early to bed them down, but with fresh water and lush grass they weren't likely to wander far.

Tobias started to collect firewood and build a fire. Once he had some good coals going, he started making coffee. Silas walked over to the cows and started to do a quick check over of them to see if any were badly injured. James rode over to him.

"From what I can see three were trampled," James told Silas, "I can see a few that are bleeding, I've been trying to corral them together over there." James pointed over to a spot where some bushes made a natural coral and about five or six cows were standing. "I warned you this morning," he said, "you don't tempt fate."

Chapter 2

It had been decided that Jesse could make it back to the town of Trinidad where he could set the bone properly and heal enough to get home on his own. Tobias was going to escort him there and get him settled before catching up with the drive. Silas knew this was the best plan, but Jesse and Tobias were his best friends out here. With the three of them they had to spread out further to keep the cattle moving. It was slower going and certainly lonelier.

After a few days they came out of the mountains and into the flatter area of New Mexico. The weather kept warming up as they came to lower elevations. The work driving the cattle was hot and dusty. After a long day, the three men often took care of their responsibilities and went to sleep almost as soon as the sun set.

They were sitting around the campfire one evening when Silas heard a sound behind him. He looked around and saw nothing, the fire had been bright and affected his night vision. He reached over to where James was laying and nudged him. James stirred a bit and looked over at Silas.

"What is it?" James growled, but before Silas could say anything, a voice came out of the darkness.

"Hello," a deep voice from the darkness, "permission to join the fire."

"Come on in," said James. Silas noticed he was pulling his gun closer and decided to do the same. A figure came out of the darkness and approached them. He was a big man, wearing a long coat and Silas could see he was carrying two guns. He crouched down and warmed his hands.

"Thank you," said the stranger, "Names Bill Wallace. I'm a US Marshal out of Albuquerque." As he said this, he pulled his coat to one side to show a Marshal's Star pinned to his chest. Their dinner, a weak stew made from jerky, wild carrots and onions that James had found close to the camp, was still by the campfire. James offered some to Bill along with some bread. Bill ate with appreciation and then poured some coffee from the pot before rolling a cigarette and lighting it up.

Cody had been on watch with the herd and came over to the fire a little surprised to see them awake with a stranger there. James stood up, it was his turn to keep watch, so he took his saddle and walked off to get his horse. Cody sat down on his bedroll and introduced himself.

"So what are you doing in these parts?" Cody asked after the introductions were done.

"I'm looking for an outlaw," said the marshal, "he's wanted for robbing a few banks. Killed the banker at the last one."

"You are welcome to camp with us," said Cody.

"Thank you for your hospitality," said the marshal. The men bunked down and soon Silas could hear the big man snoring. Silas laid there for a bit and stared up at the stars. When he was a boy, his Pa had often showed him the constellations in the stars. He told him that if he knew them well and where they belonged in the sky he would never be lost. Tonight, here with practical strangers instead of his Pa and brother, Silas felt very lost.

The next morning came quickly; Silas had the last watch and had been up for a while when he noticed movement in the camp. He rode over to see Cody and James packing up the camp. The Marshal had already saddled his horse and was walking back to the camp. Silas noticed he had a severe limp; he was favoring his left leg. James must have noticed it too and commented on it.

"Took a bullet a while back," the marshal said, "it's still in there, bothers me a bit some mornings."

"Silas here knows all about that, don't you?" Cody said while putting his bedroll on his horse. The marshal looked over at Silas in surprise.

"The kid?" he asked.

"Yep," said Cody, nonchalantly "been shot twice. He beat Tom Lassiter in a shootout." The marshal stopped moving and looked at Silas and swore.

"You beat Tom Lassiter to the draw?" he asked Silas.

"Not really," Silas said shyly, "he was trying to shoot Cody's Pa."

"A win's a win," said the marshal, "I'm impressed kid, once you get some hair on your chest the US Marshals could use you."

"I'm a cattle man," Silas said quietly, "not really a gunfighter." Silas quickly gathered his saddle bags and put everything on his pony. The marshal grinned and kept gathering his gear.

"You said last night you're after a bank robber?" Cody said, a bit sorry he had brought up Silas' past. It seemed a sore spot, and Cody didn't mean to embarrass the kid.

"Yeah," said the Marshal, "his name's Eli Carver." He pulled a wanted poster out of his saddle bag and handed it to Cody. Silas and James walked over to look at it as well. It had a drawing of a man with a square jaw and close cropped hair. "He's robbed three banks in the last few months, killed a man in cold blood too."

"I think I know this guy!" James blurted out, "except I knew him as Sampson Jones. He used to mine down in the Superstitions."

"How well did you know him?" asked the marshal.

"Not well," said James, "spoke to him a couple of times. Rumor had it that he jumped the claim he was on."

"Good to know he has another name," said the Marshal, taking out a pencil and notepad writing the name down. "If you see him there's a reward of a thousand dollars." Silas looked at the marshal, a thousand dollars was more than he had ever seen. Got him to think that maybe being a lawman did have its benefits.

Cody looked at the sky, the sun was inching upward, it was time to get the cattle on the move. He mounted his horse and the others followed suit. They said goodbye to the marshal and got the herd moving. Silas was riding drag and had lots of time to think about what he would do with a thousand dollars.

Chapter 3

They had been on the trail for another couple of days when Tobias Kent caught up with them. He reported that a doctor in Trinidad said that they had done a good job splinting the bone and it should knit together well given time. Having Tobias back meant the drive would be a little easier with a rider on each flank.

They came up on an abandoned adobe building. There was good water there, so they decided to take a break to let the cattle get some rest. They were in the desert now and the cattle had gotten used to the cooler air up in the mountains. They were really flagging, and Tobias suggested giving them time to get used to the heat.

The building was cool inside, so they set up camp in one of the rooms. It had been a while since they had a roof over their heads, even if this one was starting to crumble, it felt different. There was some furniture inside and Cody took some time to set up a real home for them. A table, some chairs and even a couple of beds. There was some fencing that they fixed up a little to contain the cows so they could get some rest themselves.

Silas wanted to get home, but this break was real nice. He loved sitting on the fence in the evening and watching the sun set. When he was younger, he would sit with his Ma and try to name all the colors in the sunset. She could always come up with more names for colors; he was sure she was making some up. As he was watching the sky fill up with colors, he noticed some riders coming over the hill. He rushed into the Adobe to alert everyone.

Tobias and Cody came out to greet the riders while James and Silas stayed in the adobe with their rifles trained out the windows in case of trouble. As the riders got closer Silas could see that they were natives. James shifted a bit, ready to open fire. Tobias raised a hand in greeting as they came closer and the riders circled around him and Cody, sitting tall on their ponies. Tobias spoke what sounded like gibberish to Silas, and one of the men responded in the same gibberish. The men got off their ponies and started walking towards the house. As they entered, Tobias told Silas and James to put down their guns.

Tobias welcomed the men to sit on the ground in the corner of the room, and they all sat. Cody and James stood in another corner, so Silas joined them. There was a lot of animated talking in the group and finally Tobias got up and walked over to talk to his partners.

"They are Paiute," said Tobias, "I grew up near a Paiute group, they are offen good folk."

"Often?" James said, eyeing the group still sitting in the corner. They were looking over at them waiting for Tobias to return.

"This group is," said Tobias, "but they are warning us that another band nearby that have taken to attacking ranchers. Mostly young'uns tired of the white man."

"Did they say where they are?" Cody said, a little concerned.

"Somewhere 'tween here and Santa Fe," said Tobias, "Paiute tend to move around." Tobias looked over at the group and spoke again in that gibberish, Silas guessed it was Paiute talk. One of the Paiute men answered him and Tobias turned back to Cody.

"He says they are sticking to the white man's trail. I'm guessing the old Spanish." Cody let out a mild oath and looked from Tobias to James. The Old Spanish was the next leg of the journey for them, it kept them
close to water until Santa Fe where they could safely turn south.

"Not sure we can skip it," says Cody, "least not with all these cows."

"How 'bout the Old Mormon Road?" Tobias suggested.

"That's a rough trail," said James, "not as much water, especially as we get into winter."

"What do you think, Silas?" Tobias looked at the young man. He didn't have the experience of these men, but they still let him in on the discussion. Since the cattle belonged to him, he had the largest stake in this drive.

Silas took a deep breath and looked at the Paiute men again, "are they telling the truth?" he asked. Cody looked over at the men as well. They were still quietly sitting, some looking over at the group but mostly just sitting looking at the floor.

"I reckon they are honest men," Tobias shrugged, "it's hard to tell with a man you just met." Silas' Pa always told him not to be quick to judge a man. Silas thought for a minute, trying to figure what his father would say in this situation. Finally, something came to him.

"I'm thinking it's better to have water and a chance of danger than no water," Silas finally said. Cody smiled and put a hand on Silas' shoulder.

"That's probably right," Cody said. James and Tobias both agreed as well.

"I'm thinking," Silas said, "maybe we don't trust these men." The others nodded, Tobias nodded a little slower than the others. "Maybe we suggest to them we're taking the Old Mormon Road."

"I like how this kid thinks," said James with a smile. Tobias just shook his head and finally agreed that this was probably wise. He walked over to the circle of men and sat talking to them for a spell before the group all stood to leave.

It was a few more days before they decided the cows had adjusted to the heat, and they could head out again. They took them over to join the Old Spanish trail and started off to Santa Fe. Cody talked to Silas about maybe selling off some of the weaker cattle in Santa Fe, since the next leg of the journey would be long and difficult. Silas spent his days thinking on that.

After a few days on the trail, life at the Adobe was all but forgotten. They were back in the daily routine of moving the cattle toward home. Silas was a little bored and nodded off a bit when James, who was in the lead position, yelled at them. Silas looked up to see that James was pointing at a small ridge up ahead. All Silas could make out was the word "rider" and concluded there must be a rider up ahead. He came alert, and looked up to the ridge, but didn't see anything. He was riding the right flank and looked over at Cody who was on the left. Cody was looking all around.

Silas heard a whoop come from over by the ridge and suddenly about fifteen riders came over the ridge and were riding hard towards them.

"Group the cattle!" Cody shouted, pulling his rifle from his scabbard. Tobias started to push the cattle from the rear into a closer formation while James turned around and stopped the leading cattle. Soon they had a tight group of cows, but the riders were almost on top of them now. Silas could see they looked like the men they had met at the adobe. This must be the Paiute raiding group. Cody was already shooting into the group of raiders, but things were moving too fast for his aim to be any good.

Tobias pulled his rifle out and started firing as well, James and Tobias were finishing grouping the cattle, who were starting to look spooked. The Paiute were spreading out and starting to circle the group, Silas turned his horse and took aim at the man in the lead of the group coming around towards his side. He fired and watched the man crumple on his horse. Silas took his eyes off that man to reload.

Cody was riding away from the herd trying to outflank the raiders. Silas saw a pack horse riding loose towards the raiders, Jesse was wrangling the four pack horses and had obviously just let them loose. The horse broke left before the raiders caught up to it and ran around back to the herd. Some of the raiders broke from their group to follow it and Silas shot at one of them. He saw him fall and as he was reloading, he caught a glimpse of a rifle in the hands of the other rider.

Silas leaned forward onto the neck of his horse to make sure he wasn't going to be shot. This proved to be a mistake as his quick movement knocked the rifle out of his hand. He lay on his pony's neck, watching helplessly as it rolled away like the wheel of a cart. Thinking about it afterwards he remembered all he could think about at that moment was how rough the horse's mane felt against his cheek.

Silas sat up again, pulling his colt out of the holster, and fired blindly in the direction of the rider that had fired at

16

him. He missed, but James had seen what happened and put a bullet into the man. The raiders were almost all around them now and the four men were constantly moving and firing at their attackers. Silas could hear Tobias yelling something in what he assumed was Paiute talk, but it didn't seem to be working.

Silas rode closer to his cows to protect them. The Paiute riders were closing in. Every now and then one of them would fall, but they kept closing the circle. Silas felt that he was a fool for deciding that this was a good idea. Silas looked around, his group were all still up and shooting, but they looked tired.

Tobias looked up at the sky and saw something that gave him some hope. He spurred his horse towards the men, pointing at the sky and yelling something in Paiute talk. As he did, the Paiute men all turned to look at the sky. Silas noticed that he was pointing at a group of birds flying overhead. The Paiutes all cried out and turned their horses and hightailed it out of there.

Silas watched in shock as they left, riding away from what seemed to be their certain victory. As they left Tobias turned back.

"Anyone hurt?" he yelled as he rode back. Nobody answered for a second, and then Cody let him know he was fine. James let out a little sigh and slid off his horse. Tobias rode over to James and jumped off his horse next to him. James was bent over double but still on his feet, Silas assumed he wasn't hurt too badly. He and Cody rode over to see what was happening. James was throwing up onto the grass;

Tobias had a hand on his back. When James finished heaving, he stood up, looking a bit embarrassed.

"That was a bit more than I could stomach," he joked. Silas chuckled and helped James back onto his horse. The men circled around, Cody and James looking around from time to time to watch for attack.

"They won't be back," Tobias said with confidence, "Kuva." He said the last word like the men should understand and accept it.

"Ku-wha?" asked James.

"Kuva," Tobias continued, "it's the word for those birds. The ravens. They're bad luck." Silas realized then that Tobias had used the Piaute's own beliefs against them. When he pointed out the ravens, they must have thought it meant bad luck and left.

"We need to move on," said Tobias, "they will want to come back for their dead."

"So?" asked James.

"It's only right to let them bury their dead," said Tobias slowly.

"They attacked us!" James exclaimed.

"We should get out of here," Cody said, interrupting the argument, "in case they decide to try again." Tobias mounted his horse again and they started getting the cattle organized. As they were sorting everything out Silas realized that several head of cattle and Boots, the paint he had borrowed to make out of the mountains, were lying dead on the ground. Boots had been working as a pack horse since they hit more level ground, he rode over to where the horse lay. Cody saw what was happening and rode over as well.

"Emily isn't going to be pleased" Cody said looking down at the fallen horse, "she liked him."

"She did," Silas said wistfully, "I promised to care for him."

"Can't be helped," Cody sighed, getting off his horse. He stripped the paint off the gear he was carrying and threw some of it on his horse and the rest on Silas' pony.

Chapter 4

Santa Fe was an old Spanish town with narrow streets and adobe style buildings with their flat roofs and stucco walls. Silas was shocked at how big it was. They had left the cattle in an old corral that Tobias knew of close to the trail. Cody suggested they go into town and get supplies and enjoy themselves.

They didn't have much money, so Silas and Cody decided to see if they could sell a couple dozen head of cattle. They asked around town if anyone was buying and met up with a rancher in a saloon who said he might be interested. The rancher came out to look at the cattle and offered eight dollars a head. Cody tried to negotiate a better price, but the man said for more money he would want to select the best of the herd. Most of them were looking thin from the trail, even after a stop at the abandoned ranch.

Silas finally agreed to eight dollars, since he wanted to get the best stock home. That made it almost two hundred dollars total. Cody and Silas did some figuring on supplies needed and that left them with enough left over to give each man ten dollars and some left over for further supplies up the trail. They were only halfway to Goldfield and still had another month at least on the trail.

After all this Silas was happy, ten dollars in his pocket in this town seemed an invitation to adventure. Tobias had come from near Santa Fe and knew his way around town, so he offered to act as their guide. Cody and Silas agreed to go with him, but James was only interested in eating and drinking his ten dollars. The three men hit the town to explore.

As they walked toward the plaza, Silas noticed a tailor shop. He looked down at his own clothes; his Ma had made his britches a while back and he was getting tall for them. When he had left home, he was barely four foot six and had grown. Mrs. Locke had made him a couple of shirts before he left but they were stained with the dust from the trail. New clothes would be a real treat! Silas told his companions he was going to go into the tailor shop. Cody gave Tobias a grin and told Silas they would meet him at the saloon when he was done. Tobias gave him directions to where to meet and then Silas was on his own. He went into the store.

An hour later he had a few dollars less and his very own broadcloth suit. He had bought something more suitable for the trail as well but felt like he fit in here with the suit. He walked to the saloon with his head held high, greeting people who went by like a gentleman. He found the saloon where he was to meet Cody and Tobias and entered. He saw his friends sitting at a table with plates of food and drinks, so he went over to join them. Cody looked up at him and a big smile went across his face.

"Kent, I think we are in the presence of a gentleman rancher," Cody said. Tobias looked up and shook his head.

"You mebbe right," Tobias said grinning, "an awful skinny one, he needs some steak!" Tobias waved down one of the saloon girls. Silas sat down at the table and grinned.

"I've never had a real suit before," he said, "I probably shouldn't have got it."

"You deserve something," said Cody, "it's been a long drive so far." Silas heard a woman's voice behind him asking what he would like. He turned and saw an absolute vision of beauty. She was about his height, brown hair tied up fashionably, but her dress is what really caught the eye. It was pink satin and clung to her tightly, her bosom was almost spilling out of the top. Silas swallowed hard, he could feel his face turning red and wasn't sure what to say.

"I believe this gentleman needs some red meat," said Tobias with a laugh, "we aim to fatten him up some before he hits the trail." Silas looked over at Tobias and scowled at him. Silas had never seen Tobias after having some whiskey, he was a little more fun when relaxed by alcohol. Silas turned back to the saloon girl and tried to smile.

"Yes please, ma'am," he said weakly, "I would like steak and some whiskey." Silas was never much of a drinker but hoped asking for some whiskey would make him look more manly. As she walked away, Silas watched the sway of her hips and had to look back at his friends before his thoughts went too far.

"This is some fancy Saloon," Silas said, trying not to think of the girls working there, but rather appreciating the room. The walls were plastered and painted deep green, the beams had fancy carving on them and even the chairs had some padding.

"It is fancy," said Cody, "Kent here recommended it. Here I had you figured for a run of the mill Cowpoke, but you like the fine life."

"This saloon hires the perty girls," said Tobias looking appreciatively around the room. The three friends continued laughing and joking as Silas' meal came and was quickly devoured. For Silas it was really the first time he was truly able to forget the loss of his father and brother. He has found some people that made him feel like part of a family again.

After eating and drinking, Silas' stomach was full, and head was light. The three men were a little unsteady on their feet, as they walked out. Silas tripped on a chair and landed in the arms of the girl in the pink satin. As she helped him back on his feet he tried to thank her but couldn't.

"Don't worry," Cody said with a grin, "I won't tell my sister you're falling for other girls." Cody and Tobias laughed at his embarrassment as they finally made it to the street. The fresh air helped them regain some of their senses and sobered them up a little. They decided to find a hotel so they could sleep in a real bed for a night. As they walked past a smaller saloon, they heard some shouting coming from inside. One of the voices sounded like James. Cody looked in and informed them it was James, and it looked like he was in trouble.

The three men entered the saloon; it wasn't as fancy as the one they just left. It had bare walls colored yellow by years of tobacco smoke, roughhewn tables and chairs and sawdust on the floor. James was standing at a table where there had obviously been a poker game going on. He had a good-sized pile of cash in front of him, so obviously his luck had been good. It was immediately obvious that one of his opponents thought his luck had been too good.

"I know a cheat when I see one!" the man across the table from James was standing and shouting at him.

"I'm no cheat!" James retorted, "you're just a lousy player." This seemed a little too insulting for the other man who reached for his gun. James' hand slapped his holster too, but as he was bringing up his gun the other man had already fired. James stumbled back and sat on the floor, blood coming from his chest.

Cody ran over, grabbing his kerchief and putting it to his chest trying to stop the bleeding. Silas stepped towards the man that shot James. He was going for his gun, but Tobias put a hand on his to stop him. Tobias pointed over at a man with a badge on his chest who was standing by the door. A deputy must have been nearby and heard the commotion.

The deputy asked what had happened and a few of the men described the whole incident. James slumped a bit lower and let out a few raspy breaths before letting out his last. Cody gently laid him down on the ground and swore.

<h1 style="text-align:center">Chapter 5</h1>

The next three days were long. Tobias helped arrange a proper funeral for James Smith. Cody worked with the Sheriff to try and bring his shooter to justice. The consensus was it was a fair shootout, so the killer could claim it was self-defense. Silas felt that wasn't fair, but some long discussions with Cody helped him realize that the law wasn't always fair.

After James was buried, they all got together to share a drink in his memory. They sat in the saloon and shared stories about James. There were a few lighter moments as they remembered him, but the mood was mostly very somber. Cody and Tobias had known him for longer, so they did most of the recounting of stories. After a little while they all sat and drank in silence.

"We do need to decide where to go from here," Cody finally said. "We have at least a month ahead of us before we get to Goldfield. We are down two men; we need to hire some more men."

"I think so," said Silas, seriously. "I'm sorry to be so much trouble for you.

"What?" Tobias looked at Silas with a slightly confused expression.

"You're driving my cattle back for me," Silas said by way of explanation, "you don't work for me or the Lazy K." The Lazy K, being the brand Silas' father had registered. It now belonged to Silas, but at this point it was just him, his Ma and about two hundred head of cattle.

Tobias looked over at his young friend. "I work for Cody's Pa, and he asked me to ride herd with you. That's enough for me to be considered working for you." Tobias then laid a hand on Silas' shoulder, "but you're a man to ride the trail with, and I'm proud to call you friend."

Silas looked from Tobias to Cody, who was nodding agreement. "He's right," Cody said, "I watched you back in the valley when we were fighting the men that stole your cattle in the first place. You were hurt and laid there in the dirt shooting back. You're a tough'un and that's no lie."

"Thank you," Silas said to him, "that means so much to me. So how do we go about getting more men?"

"We will put word out that we need two men to ride with us to Arizona," Cody said.

"That's better than trying to do it with only three of us," said Silas thoughtfully. Tobias agreed as well so they walked up to the barkeep and asked him if they could make an announcement. The barkeep agreed and Cody stood up by the bar and got everyone's attention.

"We're looking for some men to drive a herd from here to Arizona." Cody announced, "We'll be riding hard with a small crew. Pay is forty dollars when the job is done." There was some mumbling in the crowd. "Pass the word and we'll be at the corral south of town tomorrow morning. First to satisfy us will be heading out the day after."

After making the announcement, the men went to several saloons to make the same announcement. They had very little money left and decided to camp out at the corral that night to save some money. While sleeping in a bed was a nice change, Silas preferred sleeping under the stars.

The next morning Silas woke up to the familiar sound of his cattle lowing. He lay there for a second and stared at the blue sky, there were some clouds wafting by and Silas watched them go. He thought back over the last few days and how much he appreciated Tobias and Cody for standing by him, even when things got difficult. As Silas got up, he noticed that Cody was up and talking to someone who was standing at the entrance to the corral. The man was about average height, slim with a curly mop of blond hair. He had a friendly face and looked to be about eighteen years old. Silas got up to walk over.

"Silas," Cody said as Silas walked over to him, "this is Hank Coghlin. He's interested in taking the job." Silas shook hands with the man. "This is Silas, he's the owner."

"Nice to meet you," said Hank, "people mostly call me Curly."

"Good to meet you Curly," said Silas, "you have experience?"

Curly nodded his head and smiled, "I've ridden the trail a time or two, fact I just drove about five hundred head up from Phoenix. I was on my way home when I heard about this job. Ain't nothing wrong with making some money on the way home." Silas looked at Cody who was smiling.

"I think he'll do," Silas said to Cody. Cody quickly agreed and the three men shook on it.

"We head out at first light tomorrow," said Cody.

"I'll make camp with you tonight," Curly said, "make things easy." Cody took Curly over to where Tobias was fixing some coffee and bacon and introduced them. Silas rolled up his bedroll and put on his gun belt.

It was a few hours before anyone else showed. Silas was starting to think they would be a four-man crew again, when he spotted someone riding in from town. Silas noticed he was an older man, probably in his thirties and big. He was riding a big horse and made it look like he was riding a pony.

When he got up to the corral the rider got off his horse and took off his hat. He didn't have a lick of hair on his head and his skin looked like tanned leather.

"Morning sir," he said to Silas. Silas had never had someone that old call him "sir" before but responded.

"Names Zeke," the big man said slowly, "I need work."

"Let's go talk to my partner," Silas said. He led the big man over to where Cody and Tobias were sitting in the afternoon sun. Cody looked up at the big man and let out a whistle. He stood up and the man still towered over him. Tobias stood too, a little intimidated to be sitting so close to this giant.

"Who's this?" Cody asked Silas.

"Say's his name's Zeke," Silas said, "he's here about the job."

"Is that right?" Cody turned to Zeke, "you're looking for work?"

"Name's Zeke," the man said again, "I need work." Silas looked at him, he seemed a bit slow, but he knew he wanted work. Cody smiled up at the man.

"You ever been on a cattle drive?" Cody asked.

"Uh-huh." said Zeke.

"Who with?" asked Tobias after a moment of waiting for more from the man.

"Bar X" Zeke responded.

"I know of that outfit," said Tobias, "they're good. Why don't you work for them anymore?"

"Sold out." Silas guessed that meant the Bar X had sold out and he was out of work.

"You know this is a short trip?" Cody asked.

"I need work," said the big man. The three friends excused themselves and walked a little way so they could discuss hiring this man. They argued back and forth for a bit, Tobias against hiring him, Silas for and Cody wasn't sure. They finally decided to give the man a try.

After learning he was hired, Zeke gave them a big grin. He promised to be back at first light and got back up on his horse. "I think we'll need to stock up on more food," said Tobias as he watched Zeke ride off.

Chapter 6

Having five men instead of four was easier on the trail. Curly made the evenings a lot more entertaining, he loved to tell stories and shared all the stories he had heard over the years about different gunfighters. When he found out that Cody was the son of the famous Appalachian Kid, he was in awe.

Zeke was constantly there when he was needed. He might have been a bit slow, but the man knew cattle. He would look at the cows and say, "cows thirsty," or "cows tired" and the others learned to trust his read on the cows. He was one of the best cattle men Cody had ever met.

One night after they had been on the trail for a few days, they were sitting around the fire finishing up some rabbit stew and bread. They still had some fresh food from Santa Fe, but that would dry up soon and it would be back to what they could find on the trail. Curly stretched his legs out in front of him and looked at the group, they were expecting a story from him.

"Ever heard of Lightening Lassiter?" Curly started.

"You mean Tom Lassiter?" Cody asked, a little taken aback, "never heard him called 'Lightning'."

"Yeah," said Curly, "his Christian name was Tom, but people called him 'Lightning' because his draw was so fast. I heard once that he shot two men before either one could draw."

Silas looked over at Cody, and decided to say something before Cody could, "my brother saw that. Said his draw was like a blur."

"Well last I heard he had taken in with a rustler, stealing cows and that," Curly continued, "heard they stole a guy's whole ranch from under him and left."

"I heard that too," said Silas. Cody was looking at him with a sly grin.

"Ever hear the rest of that story?" Cody asked.

"No," Curly said, "have you?"

"Of course I have," said Cody. "He and that rustler got into a fight with my Pa."

"The Appalachian Kid?" Curly asked, eyes wide.

"Yep," said Cody, "Lassiter and two men ambushed him in the woods, Pa shot all three of them and got away with only a scratch." Curly was up in a crouch now, leaning forward. He loved gunslinger stories, and this one came from the son of one of them.

"But that didn't end it," Cody said, "Lassiter survived." Curly was really intrigued at this point, "The son of the rancher Lassiter murdered ended up killing Lassiter and saving the Appalachian Kid in the process."

Curly's jaw dropped to the floor when he heard that. After looking at them for a second, he said, "you're joshing me." Cody was really enjoying this, and he was proud of his friend.

Silas was about to stand up and leave when Tobias said "leave the kid alone. You can see he's embarrassed." Silas looked over at Tobias with a grateful look. Curly couldn't follow what was happening and looked from Tobias to Cody. "He's talking about the kid." Tobias said, "Silas here shot Lannister" Curly let out an oath.

"Your Pa's dead?" Zeke asked quietly. He was lying on his bedroll with his hat down over his eyes. Silas assumed he was asleep and was surprised when he spoke.

"Out of that, that's what stuck?" Curly asked.

"You need a Pa," said Zeke sitting up, his hat falling into his lap. He had a very sad look on his face. "My Pa was good, was your Pa good?"

"Yes Zeke, my Pa was good." Silas said.

"My Pa died," said Zeke, "I'm sorry about your Pa. That's sad."

"That it is," said Tobias. Zeke laid back down and put his hat back over his eyes. The rest of the men at the campfire sat quietly looking at each other. Zeke rarely added much to their campfire conversations.

That night Silas had the nightmare again. Tom Lassiter lying dead with his mother crying over him. When he startled awake, he was a bit surprised to feel a huge hand on his back. He turned to see Zeke sitting next to him, with a hand on his back.

"Bad dream," Zeke whispered.

"Yeah," Silas said.

"You need a Pa," Zeke said. He patted Silas on the back and sat there next to him while he lay there. There was something comforting in having the big man sit over him. He did need a Pa, Silas thought. He had loved spending time with his Pa on the range. His Pa had taught him everything he needed to know to be a cattleman. Life was a little different now that he was on his own.

After a fitful sleep, Silas sat up to see Cody walking over to him. "Silas," Cody said hesitantly, "if you don't want me to tell people about you shooting Lassiter, I won't."

Silas looked at his friend and said, "I wasn't thinking when I shot him, I just acted when I saw him draw."

"Pa mentioned that has happened to him," Cody said, "he says it's saved his life a few times. I saw your hand go to your gun when James was shot. What would you have done if Tobias didn't stop you?"

"Probably shot him," said Silas, "I'm not sure."

"Pa always said you need to be sure," Cody said, "killing a man isn't always the answer."
Silas picked up his bedroll and saddle bags and carried them over to his horse. He didn't have a Pa, but at least he had some friends.

As they got the herd moving again, Silas looked around at the men, two he knew very well, and two he barely knew. His mind kept going back to the day James had died. He had been so happy, buying new clothes and looking at beautiful women. They had left James to go have fun; he couldn't help but wonder what would have happened if he had stayed with James or insisted that James come with them.

He looked over at Zeke and wondered what he would think of the whole thing. Cody had mentioned that Zeke was simple-minded, maybe something had happened to him as a child and his brain never quite grew up. Silas knew he was a hard worker; he was the first in his saddle and last out with the cows after they were bedded down. One thing Silas did know about the man is that he seemed to care, he cared for the animals, and he cared for his friends. Zeke probably wouldn't have let James go off on his own.

Chapter 7

"Rider coming," Curly yelled over the moving cattle. Curly was in the lead today and so was first to see the lone rider coming towards them. As the rider got closer, Silas could see him from his place on the right flank. He didn't look like he was doing too good, he was only holding his reins with one hand, the other was clenched to his right side. His hat was dangling behind him, held on by the chinstrap, even though the sun was high overhead.

When he came alongside Curly, he almost fell off his horse. Curly held him up as the rest of the men stopped the herd and moved closer to see what was happening. "He's hurt bad," Curly shouted as they got closer. Zeke was one of the first men to reach them and lifted the rider over to his horse, supporting him so he didn't fall off. He then rode over to where some trees were giving some shade.

Tobias and Curly went with him and helped get the rider to the ground. Tobias looked at his face and stood up straight. "It's Bill Wallace!" he said before bending over the man to see if he could find the problem.

"Who's Bill Wallace?" Curly asked.

"He's a marshal," Silas said, "looking for a bank robber when we crossed paths."

"He's been wounded," Tobias grunted, trying to move the big man around. "No blood, but he's bruised up something fierce."

"Beating," said Zeke.

"What?" asked Cody.

"That's beating," Zeke explained in his simple manner. "They beat him." Silas looked down at the marshal and that is what he looked like, it looked like several men had beaten him to an inch of his life.

"The giant's right," Bill managed to groan. Cody looked off into the distance and saw a dust cloud over the horizon.

"They still coming for you?" Cody asked.

"Likely," said Bill. Silas rode his horse over to the cattle and looked to the horizon. From this vantage point he could see the riders coming.

"More riders," he yelled over "maybe ten or fifteen." Silas noticed that there was a spring nearby, there was a pool of water, but it's obvious that at some time of the year there is enough water to fill a pond. The hollow was a good size. He rode back over to the tree and suggested they move the cattle into the hollow and hunker down in there. Zeke got moving while the others still talked through better locations to hide. They were in an open plain so there weren't many places. Cody rode over to help Zeke and Silas herd the cattle, while Curly and Tobias helped the marshal to walk the few steps into the hollow. Curly moved the three horses and their pack horses and staked them close to the water.

Once the cattle were settled and enjoying the sudden reprieve from the long walk, the coming riders were much closer. Silas took position laying on a slight incline into the hollow, his rifle in his hands. He could now see the riders clearly and could get an accurate count. There were thirteen men, all armed and all looking ready to fight.

Curly ran over to him, bent low so he wasn't an easy target. He laid down next to Silas and looked over at him, his face concerned. "Don't tell the others," Curly said quietly, "but I've never been in a gunfight." Silas looked at him, now the obsession with gunfighters made sense. After being in a few fights, they become something to avoid, not admire. Silas also felt a strange sense of responsibility toward the man, compared to the older man, Silas was a seasoned gunfighter.

"We'll be ok," he said quietly, "Tobias and Cody are the best." Silas looked over at his two friends who were lying next to each other on a different part of the incline. They were talking, likely figuring out some strategy. Silas had seen them take on the cattle rustlers that had ambushed them when they were trying to get his cattle back. They disappeared up a mountain slope and came back a while later, having killed or run off all the men.

Zeke was back with the marshal and the cattle, his gun was drawn, and he had a serious look on his face. Silas couldn't help but think of the stories Emily once told him about a mama bear protecting its cubs. Heaven help anyone that hurt anyone Zeke decided to protect. Now he was thinking about Emily, he wondered where she was right now. Probably helping her Ma with making grub for her family. Or maybe at the barn, tending to the horses. Hopefully she was thinking of him and her brother and saying a prayer.

The riders were close enough to see the features on their faces now. Silas shook his head to clear his thoughts. He looked over to see that Cody was moving over to the marshal. Silas was hoping the riders would move on without seeing them, but of course that would be impossible. Even just two hundred head of cattle were hard to miss. As the riders started to approach, obviously expecting trouble, Cody stood up, both hands in the air. Silas sighed, of course he would try talking.

"Hello!" Cody shouted. "How can we help you?" He sounded friendly like he was inviting them to sit and have tea with them.

"We're after that marshal!" One of the men shouted.

"I spoke with the marshal," Cody said matter of factly, "he said he'd rather stay away from you." The man who had shouted swore. "In fact, he just told me how you are not very hospitable people." Cody almost had a smile on his face; he sounded like he was enjoying himself. Silas knew Cody's Pa sometimes used big words when squaring off because it confused people.

"You're outnumbered," said the rider.

"Likely," said Cody, "I've seen worse. I would bet some of you can't even shoot straight." Silas suddenly realized what was going on, Cody was distracting the men while Tobias crawled around the men on his belly. Silas only knew this because Tobias was nowhere to be seen. That was the only logical solution. Silas indicated to Curly that he should stay here and snuck around as best he could to a place a little further out.

The riders were starting to get antsy and got real nervous when Cody shouted "now!" and dropped down to the ground. The riders' horses all danced around a bit as their owners tried to figure out what was going on. Nothing happened. Silas laughed a bit and to himself, he watched Curly, who was a bit confused, bring his rifle to bear.

Silas near jumped out of his skin when Cody crawled up to him and whispered, "Kent should be finished by now, we can let 'em have it." Cody raised his rifle and shot into the riders; he missed but it gave the riders some focus. Silas fired as well and grazed one of the riders. He watched him falter and pull himself back up. Curly heard them fire and opened fire himself. He had been very focused on finding a good target and one of the riders slumped off of his horse.

Cody moved over between Silas and Curly and fired again, this time finding a target. Silas managed to get off a good shot as well. Curly wasn't as lucky this time, but the riders were fighting back now, and he had to duck his head as he fired. Cody whistled and Silas heard a whistle in return.

Cody waved to Curly and Silas to follow him and rushed over to the horses. The others followed him, all bent low as the riders fired. Cody beckoned to Zeke to join them, and he did. Cody said, "let's ride at them, see if we can get them to run. Fire into them with your pistols. Create chaos." Cody was smiling.

They mounted up and spurred their horses up out of the hollow firing and yelling like they were loco. There were only ten riders left on their horses and one of them was wounded. They were not expecting to see four crazed men riding at them and all turned their horses. Silas couldn't help but wonder how this would work. It wouldn't take long for them to realize they could win easily and turn back.

Silas' jaw nearly hit the floor when the horses in front of them all tripped up, throwing most of the riders to the ground. Silas stopped his horse short and so did his companions. They had an upper hand now that he was not expecting. Cody had somehow planned this, and he was riding at one of the men who managed to stay astride his horse, he used his upper body to push the man down while he was still off balance. Zeke saw this and decided to do the same with another man, except the man had regained his balance. Zeke pushed hard and the two of them fell, Zeke landing on the other man. There was a sickening crunch of bones, and the rider yelled in pain.

Tobias appeared out of nowhere, right next to the final rider who had maintained his balance and pushed one foot up out of the stirrups and kept pushing until the man fell off. With all the men on the ground, Silas, Cody and Curly surrounded the men with their pistols pointed at them. Most of the men were unarmed now and put their hands up in surrender. The few that had held on to weapons, were fast to drop them. Zeke was up and helped Tobias collect as many fallen guns as they could find.

"Marshal Wallace tells me you're the Thornback Gang." Cody said, Curly turned to look at Cody in shock. Silas had heard that name too, but it didn't really mean much to him. To him outlaws were outlaws. "I suppose we've just caught you," Cody continued.

"That was some nasty trick," said one of the Thornback men.

"You had us outnumbered," said Tobias with a shrug, "we had to do something." Silas looked down and saw that Tobias had used his lasso to make a trip line. In the confusion the gang didn't see anything, and the horses tripped up, allowing them to get caught. It was a sneaky thing to do. They gathered the gang together and tied their hands behind them with strips of rawhide. After getting them all lined up they marched them over to the spring where Marshal Wallace was looking at them in shock. He slowly stood up and walked down the line of men, looking each one in the face.

"Long's not here," the marshal said.

"Flint Long?" Curly asked. Silas was impressed at his ability to know the names of all the gunfighters and outlaws.

"He got hit," said one of the gang members. "First thing." Silas thought for a moment, the first one down was shot by Curly. He wondered if Curly managed to shoot the leader of the Thornback Gang.

"The reward is five hundred dollars," said the marshal, "dead or alive." Silas was shocked. Curly has just earned five hundred dollars. It's possible he didn't even realize it yet.

"Congratulations Curly," Silas blurted out.

"What?" Curly asked.

"If Long went down first," Silas pointed out, "then the reward is yours." Cody came over and clapped curly on the shoulder; Tobias offered a sincere congratulations. Curly just stood there looking around.

"Five hundred dollars?" Curly said slowly, "I've never had five hundred dollars." The marshal took him by the hand and shook it.

Chapter 8

Trying to keep prisoners and drive cattle seemed foolish. The marshal was bruised but able to ride. Cody and Silas spent some time talking with the marshal and they decided he should ride the prisoners on to Albuquerque. Tobias and Curly could go with him to help control the prisoners and Curly could claim his reward.

The night before they left, Marshal Wallace told them what had happened to him that day. He heard that Carver, the bank robber he was chasing, had been working with the Thornback gang. Wallace tracked the gang for weeks before finding them in an abandoned ranch house a few miles off. When he got there, he tried to sneak around the house to see who was inside when two of the gang members jumped him. They dragged him inside and tied him to a chair. They asked him who he was chasing after, but he didn't answer so they decided to beat it out of him.

During the beating, he managed to get untied and fight back. He fought hard enough to escape the house and get to his horse. The Thornback men wanted him dead, so they chased after him. He was barely conscious when he spotted the dust from the cattle and rode over to see if he could get help. He was very glad he came across friendly folk.

As the three men led the prisoners out the next morning, Silas was happy to see them go. The whole night, they had to take shifts guarding them. The outlaws also took shifts cussing out their guards. Silas couldn't see the back of them soon enough. They should be in Albuquerque by sunset. His group would be a day or two behind them.

If Silas thought Santa Fe was a sight, Albuquerque was something else. Wide streets and fancy saloons everywhere. They had a lot of ranches moving cattle through to ship north on the railroad, so there was plenty of accommodation for his cattle. Silas and Cody picked a stock pen that would let him keep his herd there for two dollars a day, or four if they wanted grain. Silas decided it might be good to give them two days of rest and grain to give them energy for the last stretch. They had maybe twenty-five days before the cows would finally be home.

After getting the herd settled, Silas, Cody and Zeke went over to the Highland Hotel. Tobias had suggested it was a good place to meet back up. Silas thought of the girls at the last place Tobias had chosen. He wondered if this place had pretty girls too. They got to the three-story hotel; Silas couldn't believe the size of it. Zeke seemed a little afraid of it as well. He wasn't used to any sort of luxury, much less a dollar a night hotel. They walked into the dining hall of the hotel and were amazed at the luxury. Padded seats, curtains hanging from the walls, and shiny dark wood everywhere. Silas was happy he still had that fancy suit, or he would not fit in here. Curly was sitting at one of the tables with a fancy China cup in front of him.

Curly waved them over, "you made it!" Curly said happily. Can you believe this place?" Curly pointed around the room. "I could get used to having real cash money." They sat with Curly, and he told them how they got to the US marshal's office two days before and locked the prisoners up. Marshall Wallace had given him the five-hundred-dollar reward when another marshal looked at the men in the cells.

"You've got Slim Tom in here too," the marshal had told Wallace. Wallace looked him up in his book and told them to come back the next day.

"Would you believe it," Curly said finishing his story, "another five hundred dollars for Slim Tom! That's a hundred dollars each." Silas looked at Cody, he didn't think that was fair since Cody and Tobias had the plan, they should get the money. Cody had a huge smile on his face.

Cody slapped Zeke on the back and said "Zeke how about that? A hundred dollars!" Zeke just frowned at them. He wasn't used to padded chairs and fine China and now he was richer than he'd ever been. He didn't know what to say. Silas was glad for Zeke that Tobias chose that moment for his grand entrance. He was dressed like a dandy, blue broadcloth suit, satin shirt and new Plains hat on his head. Up until now he had worn a muslin shirt, wool coat and beat up sombrero. Silas barely recognized him.

"Now who's the gentleman?" Silas joked as Tobias walked over to them.

"Did Curly tell you the news?" Tobias asked.

"Sure did," Cody said, "a hundred dollars, good to see the money hasn't changed you." Cody, being the son of a successful rancher, was used to having money. He was enjoying watching the others with newfound fortune. The five men ate a hearty dinner of stewed pork with fresh bread and apple pie. They were so full they almost couldn't move to go to their rooms.

Silas' room wasn't as fancy as the dining hall, but it had a chair, bed, side table with a washing basin and a wardrobe. Silas took his suit out of the saddle bag to hang out some of the wrinkles. He was looking forward to wearing it the next day. He had been given his share of the reward money, and he put it in his boot. As he washed himself in the basin, feeling weeks of dust coming off there was a knock on the door.

He opened the door to find Zeke there, filling the entire entryway. Silas invited Zeke in, Zeke came in and sat awkwardly on the chair while Silas sat on the bed. Zeke still looked a little lost.

"How can I help you?" Silas asked. Zeke looked a little sheepish, which was hard for a man that big.

"You have no Pa," he started, "I have no Pa."

"That's right," said Silas, wishing a little that Cody was here. Cody had built a rapport with Zeke, and Silas sensed he might need help in explaining whatever it was Zeke needed to explain.

"That makes us like brothers." Zeke continued.

"Brothers?" Silas had to think on that, "I guess so. You're a good man Zeke, and I'd like to have a brother like you. You take good care of the animals and your friends." Zeke smiled at this and then the smile faded.

"I'm not smart," Zeke said after a moment's pause. "I don't know what to do with a hunnerd dollars."

"You know how to handle money, don't you?" Silas was a bit confused, surely this man had been paid off after cattle drives. That's usually a good amount of money.

"Yes," Zeke said thoughtfully, "but not a hunnerd dollars."

"It's a bit much at once?" Silas thought he was getting the idea now.

"Uh-huh," Zeke nodded. "Can I let you hold it?"

"You want me to take care of it?" Silas asked, "why me? Why not Cody or Tobias? They're older."

"You have no Pa," Zeke said as if that explained everything.

"Right," Silas was lost again. He liked Zeke, but talking to him could be difficult. "I'll hold onto it for you. If you want to buy something, new clothes or boots or anything I'll help you with buying it. Does that sound good?"

Zeke smiled and nodded. He seemed legitimately relieved as he pulled the cash from his pocket and handed it to Silas. Silas took the cash and slipped it into his pocket. He would put it in the other boot later. He wasn't even going to let Zeke know his hiding place.

As they walked to the door Zeke stopped again and looked at Silas. "These are fancy beds," he said looking back at Silas' bed.

"Yes, they are," Silas said patiently.

"They don't feel right." Zeke said thoughtfully, "do they mind if we sleep on the floor?"

"I reckon not," Silas answered, "you paid for the whole room. You can use it however you want." Zeke smiled and walked out of the room, thanking Silas for everything. Silas grinned as he put the money in his other boot. Laid down with his hands behind his head and looked up at the ceiling, it only took a minute, and he was asleep.

The next day the five men met at breakfast. Fresh eggs, biscuits with gravy and steak were a treat after hardtack and black coffee. Silas ate enough for two men before sitting back and looking around the room. There were a lot of ranchers there, a few of them had brought their wives. Albuquerque was a busy town; a lot of cattle being sold to go north or to feed the army. Silas fit right in wearing his suit, he even felt that it was still wrinkled was a good thing. It showed he's had money for a while.

They all had different ideas about what to do in town. Silas had noticed that Zeke's boots were getting old, his toes were poking through the boots as he walked. He suggested they go boot shopping. Tobias was thinking about going to a dance hall and Curly decided to join him. Cody went to a bathhouse to give himself a good cleaning.

Silas and Zeke tried a couple of stores only to find nobody had boots big enough for Zeke's large feet. In the third store the lady behind the counter suggested they go to the old Spanish town where there was a quality boot maker. She told them it might cost a little more, but he could get made to measure boots.

The streets narrowed as they hit the Old Spanish part of town, and the buildings went from wooden storefronts to adobe. Silas and Zeke followed the shopkeeper's directions to a building with "Jose Jiminez, Boots" painted on a sign outside. They walked inside and were immediately greeted with the smell of tanned leather.

An older Mexican man met them as they came in. He had grey hair and a small mustache. He greeted them with a big smile and showed them around the ready-made boots available. There were none the right size for Zeke.

"I can make some," the bootmaker told them. "I'm not so busy now, maybe take me a day. It would be a costly thing," the bootmaker added, "I think maybe too much money. I can't give any discount."

"How much?" Silas asked.

"Let me measure," said the man. He got out a tape and started to take all the measurements. After doing some calculations he told them they would be eighteen dollars. Silas took Zeke aside and asked him if he was willing to spend that much on boots.

"How much would be left?" Zeke asked seriously.

"I figure about eighty dollars," Silas said. Zeke's eyes got huge. He obviously wasn't good at figures. Maybe it was good that Silas was helping him.

"I can buy fancy boots and have money left?" Zeke asked.

Silas had a sudden realization, "how did you get boots that fit before?"

"Pa gave me his," Zeke said seriously. Silas thought about times he had gotten new boots. They had always been inexpensive ones from the general store, but they were new. He really felt sorry for his big friend.

Silas turned to the bootmaker and said, "he'll take them." Silas watched Zeke look around at the boots on the shelves and had an idea. "Put his initials on them," he said so Zeke couldn't hear, He told the bootmaker the initials, who wrote it down. He knew that would cost extra, but he would make up the difference with his own money.

The group had decided to meet at a saloon for lunch. Lunch on the trail was usually eaten while riding, not wanting to lose daylight. Curly has been to Albuquerque once before and had suggested a saloon he knew well. Zeke and Silas were the first to arrive and found a table. This saloon had a table where they could help themselves to roast beef, stew and bread. Zeke loaded his plate down, and Silas ordered them some drinks.

The other three men were there shortly after. They sat at the table and Curly told them all about the dance hall girls they watched that morning. Silas appreciated beautiful women but thought he would be too embarrassed to just sit and stare at them. Zeke told the men that he bought some fancy boots, which Cody and Tobias congratulated him for. It was turning out to be a fine meal with men that had become good friends on the trail.

Silas decided to treat the men to another drink and walked over to the bar to order a bottle of tequila for the table. He was a little lightheaded after a drink himself, and decided he was done drinking, but he wanted to be kind to his older friends who were more used to drinking.

At the bar he was approached by a man who had two guns on his waist. He stood a good foot taller than Silas and looked down at him with some disdain. He just towered over him and blocked him from going back to his table. Silas looked up at the man and frowned.

"Excuse me," Silas said to the man, but he didn't move. Silas tried to push by him, but the man wouldn't let him pass. "What do you want?" Silas finally asked.

"I hear you're the one that brought in the Thornback gang," the man finally said.

"My crew did," Silas said, "what's that to you?"

"But I heard word that you are also the one that shot Lightning Lassiter," Silas looked at the man hard. He wasn't sure how this man had heard this, but figured Curly was telling his stories around town. The stories were true, so that didn't bother him much. Men trying to build a reputation fighting him might be a problem though.

"I don't see how that's any of your business," Silas said quietly.

"I don't reckon how a pipsqueak like you kin beat a man like Lassiter," said the man. This irked Silas a little, but he wasn't about to pick a fight. He had seen James Smith lose a similar fight and wasn't cocky enough to think he wouldn't have the same luck.

"It was luck," Silas said, "now please let me get back to my friends." The gunfighter pushed Silas back and squared off. Silas got ready to draw. His hand was on his colt, and he was bringing it up when the gunfighter crumpled to the ground.

Silas took a minute to register that Zeke was standing where the gunfighter had been, an empty bottle in his hand. Silas looked at the gunfighter laying out cold on the floor. Zeke gave him a sheepish smile and turned to go back to the table where the other three men were laughing.

"Friend of yours?" Tobias joked as Silas rejoined the table.

"Never met the man," Silas said, "apparently he heard I killed Lassiter and wanted to fight." Curly looked a bit embarrassed, realizing he had been the one to tell people about Silas' exploits. "I guess it was bound to happen," Silas said. He had heard of men that got a reputation for gunfighting without really wanting to. He now realized this actually could happen.

They looked over at the man that had confronted Silas, who was still unconscious on the floor. The men around him just ignored the whole situation, some of them even stepping over the body.

"We better go before he comes to," said Cody, "he will not be happy." As they walked out Silas looked over to Zeke and thanked him for stepping in. Zeke just smiled at him and put a large hand on his shoulder.

As they walked back to the hotel, Silas replayed what just happened at the saloon. What if Zeke hadn't been there? He wasn't sure if he could have beat the man to the draw. James had been fast and still ended up bleeding on the floor. He had never considered that he would need to be fast, all his life guns had been for protecting cattle from predators and hunting. Now he had a reputation.

Chapter 9

As they were getting everything ready to move the herd again, Silas was a bit surprised as Curly joined them with his gear. He had expected Curly to quit the drive, since he was now a wealthy man. Curly was a man of his word though and he had agreed to do a job.

Zeke showed up with his new boots. Silas had shown him the scrolling letters, "Z.W." that the bootmaker had expertly added to the boots. Silas didn't think that Zeke wouldn't recognize the letters and he would have to explain what they meant. Zeke had shown everyone in the crew his new boots, proudly pointing out the fancy writing.

They were close to Arizona, and it started feeling more like home to Silas. He missed his Ma, he felt guilty having snuck away, but was sure he had done the right thing. His father had started with nothing and worked hard to build a healthy herd. He finally felt they had enough to be comfortable when he had been murdered for his small herd. Silas looked over what was left, only a couple hundred head or so, but it was enough to start over. He would get home soon and fix things up with his mother. She would surely see that he had been right.

They had been on the trail for a few days when they spotted a small cabin up ahead. It was adobe with a flat roof, maybe one or two rooms. There was an empty corral next to it with a small shelter to allow animals to get out of the weather. It looked abandoned so Cody and Tobias suggested it might be nice to camp the night there. The corral would mean nobody would have to stand watch.

After securing the cows in the corral, and unsaddling
their horses, they started to head for the house when they heard
a voice coming from the house. "Hold it right there boys!" the
voice said, "I aim to shoot to kill." The five men stopped; Silas
and Tobias quickly had their guns in their hands but didn't
bring them up.

"Outlaws!" Curly hissed as he stepped backwards.
Cody slowly put his hands up, always the one to talk, he
stepped forward.

"Hello, in the house," Cody said loudly, "we thought it
was abandoned. We will keep moving on." Silas could see a
shadow in the window move; he had his target if the shooting
started.

"Do you work for Slade?" asked the voice.

"Don't know a Slade," responded Cody, "we work for
this man here, his name is Trent." They could hear some
voices coming from the house but couldn't make out what they
were saying. One voice was female. Not likely outlaws.

The shadow in the window moved and the door swung
open. A tall man walked out, rifle in his hands. He was slim
and had greying hair that had once been black. He walked over
to the men, looking at Silas.

"You're the boss?" he asked Silas.

"In a way," said Silas, "I own the cattle. The men
work for Cody's Pa; they are helping me get them home." The
man looked at the five cowboys. He finally put a hand out to
Silas, who quickly holstered his colt and shook hands.

"Names Locke," said the man, "Fred Locke. This is
my place, what's left of it."

Cody took a step forward, "you related to Henry
Locke?" he asked.

"He's a cousin," said Fred, "haven't seen him since he left home."

"I'm his oldest," said Cody, "name's Cody Locke, my Pa told me about you. He was hoping you survived the feuding."

"Left shortly after he did," said Fred, shaking his head. "Can't believe it, Henry's boy." He turned to the house and shouted "Susan! Mary! Come out here!" Two women appeared at the doorway, an older woman about as grey as Fred and a girl about fourteen or fifteen years old. Silas' heart jumped, she was the spitting image of Emily, same gold hair and same dark brown eyes. She was a whole lot thinner though, almost sickly looking.

"Meet my wife Susan, and daughter Mary," said Fred. He indicated Cody to the women, "this is our cousin, Cody Locke." Susan and Mary took turns shaking his hand. Cody took a moment to introduce everyone else. Susan invited them into the house to talk.

The house was small; it was a room with a table in the middle and a large fireplace at the far end. Each side of the room was divided off with hanging quilts. Silas could see that there were beds behind each quilt. There was a pot on a hook over the fire and Mary rushed over because whatever was in it was starting to smell burnt. There were only two chairs, but there was a bench by the table and another by the fireplace. They all sat.

They spent some time catching up on family, but there really weren't many Lockes left, so that didn't take too long. Cody told them a little bit about what got them driving cattle to Goldfield. Susan and Mary got together all the dishes they had in the house to serve up some rabbit stew. They had added some water to make it stretch so it wasn't the best, but it was appreciated.

They had been talking for a while, with the low fire putting out a fair bit of heat. Silas was getting drowsy. He was trying to keep his eyes open when he noticed there was a body sitting very close to him. He hadn't realized that Mary had squeezed in next to him. It was the only good spot in the small room, but it felt odd to have a girl sitting so close to him.

Tobias asked a question that made Silas forget the warm touch of Mary next to him. "Who is Slade?" he asked. Fred's face got very dark.

"Burton Slade," Fred said, his voice going low. "He's trying to force us off his land." Fred then went into a long story about starting out here about five years ago. He had worked as a ranch hand, and then lead hand for a while, saving up all the money he could. Susan had worked in the ranch house as well so they could save up. They had bought this land and built on it, buying a dozen head to start off on their own. It was going well until the drought hit last year and they lost everything.

Burton Slade had offered to buy the land, but only for a fraction of what it was worth. They had refused to sell, putting word out that they would sell to anyone that could give them a good price. Slade warned everyone against making an offer. He had been sending hired guns over to intimidate them. That's why he was preparing to fight any rider that came.

It was getting late, and the cattle were starting to complain. There was no good water in the corral, Zeke told everyone the cows were thirsty. Fred mentioned that there was a creek behind the house where they got water. The water in the creek was moving slowly and was brackish. They managed to carry over enough water to keep the cows happy, but it took time. Fred helped, apologizing that the spring they had fenced in had gone dry.

When they were done, they were bone tired, and the sun was setting. They made camp between the corral and the cabin. As they sat around the fire, they discussed the problems the Locke family was facing. Cody was torn.

"Silas," he finally said, "I know I promised you I would get this cattle home for you, but these people are kin. I feel I should stay and help them."

Silas thought about this for a minute then said, "of course you need to help." Cody smiled at him and thanked him for understanding. Tobias looked at Cody for a minute. He rode for the Locke family and was also torn. Cody saw his look and let him know he was free to stay with Silas. Silas took a minute to digest all of this.

"We're friends," Silas finally said, "and your family has been awfully good to me." Silas got up into a crouch, leaning toward the fire. He wanted to go home but also felt that this family needed his help. Tobias should be freed to stay and help. If Slade really was hiring gunfighters, they'd need Tobias to help.

"Tobias," Silas said, "you can make a decision, but if it were mine, I'd tell you to stay. You're a good man with a gun. The three of us can finish this drive." Curly nodded in agreement. Silas wasn't sure if Zeke was following anything, he just kept sniffing the air. Tobias looked at them, quietly he agreed that it would be best for him to stay.

The matter settled, they all bunked down for the night. Silas was having a hard time sleeping. He sat and stared at the sky. It was a full moon and the whole place was lit up almost as bright as the day, making sleep more difficult. He thought of Mary, her warm body next to him. A couple of times her arm brushed against his, he could feel the bones in her arm and her skin was rough. His mind went to Emily; they had held hands a few times. Her touch was electric, driving a passion in his heart. She was soft and delicate, while also feeling incredibly strong.

Emily would want him to stay. He felt it deep inside him, if she knew a cousin was in trouble, she would ask him to help. He would never refuse Emily, even if her request was imaginary. He saw Zeke shifting next to him.

"Zeke, you awake?" he whispered.

"Yes," the big man whispered.

"I think we should stay and help these people," Silas said.

"Good," Zeke said, "tomorrow I find water. Cows thirsty." Silas shook his head, he wasn't sure what the man meant, but having made a decision Silas was asleep in a moment.

The next morning Silas woke to find Zeke gone. He looked around the camp and the cattle but couldn't see him. His saddle and horse were gone too. "Anyone seen Zeke?" he asked. Curly and Tobias shrugged, they were fixing breakfast and over by the fire. Cody was over by the horses, so Silas went over to ask him.

"The oddest thing," said Cody, "he saddled up at first light and rode off talking about finding water."

"He mentioned that last night," said Silas.

"He should be here helping get ready to move on," Cody said quietly.

"Not really," Silas said, "I decided last night we're staying on here. I guess Zeke is going to see if he can find water, so we don't have to haul it from the creek."

"I wonder about him," Silas said, "sometimes he doesn't know what's going on, but with the cattle he understands everything." Cody smiled and shrugged. The two walked back to the fire to get some food. Silas mentioned the new plan to Curly.

"If you want to head off, I understand," Silas said.

"Leave?" Curly sounded incredulous, "and miss out watching the son of the Appalachian Kid and Short Hand Trent take on hired guns? I'm sticking around!"

"Short Hand Trent?" asked Silas.

"Yep," said Curly, "that's the name I'm giving you." Silas sighed, that was the type of name that would stick with a body. He knew he stood a fair sight shorter than other men, but he never really thought of himself as short. He had already started to outgrow the new clothes he got in Santa Fe, maybe he would end up a tall man. Curly wasn't really going to change his mind, so Silas just let it go.

Zeke came riding hard to the campfire, a huge grin on his face. "There's water," he said. The four men were surprised to hear he'd found water so quickly, since Fred said everything was dry. They saddled their horses and followed Zeke.

He led them to a dried-up pond and pointed happily at the cracked ground. The other men sighed, and Cody carefully explained the drought had dried up the spring. Zeke's face didn't change; he was still smiling.

"Under," said Zeke, "I'll dig, it's just under." The men agreed this might work and rode back to the adobe cabin. They got off their horses and started the long task of watering the cattle. Fred came out to help, seemingly happy to be doing anything to care for cattle again. While working the men told Fred their plan to stay and help. Fred was appreciative but seemed a little unsure that this was a good idea.

"We don't have any water or grass for your cattle," Fred told them.

"I dig water," Zeke said confidently.

Before Fred could respond, Silas said "and I can buy some grain. I just happened on some extra cash." Cody smiled at his friend and then looked at Fred like this solved any possible objection.

After the cattle were watered, Zeke borrowed a shovel from Fred and rode off happily. He rejected any offers of help, he was going to be able to take care of it. Cody and Fred talked over grain options. Fred mentioned there was a trading post about ten miles south of them. It would take a couple of days for the round trip with the wagon, but they couldn't carry the grain they needed without it.

It was decided that Fred would take Silas and Cody to get the grain, they would leave as soon as possible and should reach the trading post by sunset. Susan quickly put some food together for them, they didn't have much so Cody quietly supplemented the food from their supply. Fred drove the wagon while Cody and Silas rode on either side.

They left as quickly as they could and rode steady until they reached an old wooden building, surrounded by some small trees. There was a small river flowing behind the trading post, creating a lush oasis in the arid region. The sun was setting as they arrived and the trading post was closed. They set up camp close to the river and enjoyed a nice evening together. Fred was a likable man, who enjoyed telling Cody stories of what Henry Locke was like as a youth.

The trading post opened early in the morning, and Silas went in to buy as much grain as he could. He wasn't sure how long they would be there and wanted to be prepared. Cody suggested to Fred that since they were adding mouths to feed, they should also buy some dry goods. He was certain that Fred was struggling to feed his family and wanted to help without insulting his cousin. The wagon loaded they headed back to the ranch.

They were about three or four miles away from the trading post when five men on horses rode towards them on the path. They looked like they were heading to the training post and Silas expected them to ride past the wagon. Instead, they blocked the path so the wagon couldn't get through. There was one man that was a little bit older than the others, he was heavily set and clean shaven, which was a shame because a beard would have hidden his second chin. The other four riders flanked him on each side. They looked like rough men.

The big man spoke, "well it's my lucky day boys, looks like Locke here has bought us some grain."

"Now look here Slade," said Fred, "we don't want no trouble." So, this was the infamous Slade, Silas was not impressed, no wonder he hired guns, this guy didn't look like he could be any trouble in a fight. Cody rode forward and put up one hand.

"This grain belongs to my partner here," Cody said, "he doesn't take kindly to being robbed. Kindly move aside." Silas would have been surprised if that worked, but he still appreciated Cody's desire to avoid bloodshed.

"I see," said Slade, sizing up Silas. "So, you are letting a child buy your grain. Are you really that hard up?"

"I wouldn't call him a child." Cody said, giving Silas a sly look. "Why that there is Short Hand Trent," Silas shook his head, the name was going to stick now.

One of the hired guns grunted, "ain't never heard of no Short Hand Trent."

"Really?" Cody managed to sound shocked, like he didn't just hear the name yesterday. "He's the one that outdrew Tom Lassiter," that was a lie, "and helped bring the whole Thornback Gang to justice." Silas gave Cody a dirty look. Cody turned to look at him and gave him a wink that Slade couldn't see. He seemed to enjoy this type of thing, Silas decided he could do one better.

"He's one to talk," he said, indicating Cody. "You're looking at 'Dead Eye Locke' making up a name on the spot. "That's right, the first born of the Appalachian Kid. He's a better shot than his Pa too. I've seen him shoot a fly off a vulture. He can disappear into the woods and next time you see him is when you have a hole in your chest." He looked back at Cody, who was working hard not to laugh at this nonsense.

Slade looked from one to the other. "You're both full of wind," he said, "I bet you can't fight worth anything."

"You don't want to try us," Cody threatened.

"Like they said," Fred interjected, "the grain isn't mine so kindly move so I can help the lad deliver his grain." Slade had to think on this for a minute. The gun fighters behind him were getting anxious, ready for some action. Silas saw one move his hand toward his gun, and drew as fast as he could, pointing the gun at the man. With all that was going on, nobody saw him draw, it was fast but not as fast as Cody was talking up.

"Keep your hand on the pommel," Silas said to the man. He looked surprised to see a gun pointed at him, he had been looking at Cody when Silas drew on him. He slowly put his hand back on the horn of his saddle. Silas looked at the other men, "you'd all be smart to do the same."

"He's fast I tell you.," Cody said, looking a little surprised as well. "If you gentlemen don't want to die, you'd best move aside." The hired guns were looking pale at this point, but Slade was not as easily impressed or was plain stupid. Bullies often were just stupid.

Slade looked around at the men and said, "come on men, back me up here."

One of them decided to try a fast draw on Silas and learned fast that was a bad idea as Silas put a bullet into his shoulder. The gunshot spooked the horses pulling the wagon and they started forward. Silas spurred his horse forward and saw out of the corner of his eye that Cody's horse was riderless. He was sure he only heard his shot but didn't have time to worry about his friend.

Cody had slid off his horse and had run to the back of the wagon and jumped in. As the wagon lurched forward, he rushed to the seat, firing as the wagon moved forward. Slide's men were shooting back now, but in the confusion didn't really know where to aim. Cody fired and another man fell off his horse. The wagon pushed through the riders with Silas ahead clearing the way.

The men moved aside, this time getting a little better aim. Splinters flew up from the seat between Fred and Cody. Silas fired at another man and watched him drop his gun.

Grabbing at his hand. Silas hadn't aimed for the hand, but a hit is a hit.

As the Wagon made it through, Cody whistled and his horse ran to catch up with them. Silas knew Cody spent time training his horse, but this was impressive. Silas looked back to see that one of the gunfighters left standing was taking aim for him, so he fired over his shoulder. He missed but hit a tree close to the man and made him duck. This gave Silas time to aim again and hit his target this time. With all four gunfighters taken care of they could ride on safely. They were sure Slade didn't have the courage to come after them with his paid muscle so easily dispatched.

After a few minutes, they slowed down and Cody got off the wagon to remount his horse. As he hit the ground he swore. He looked down and he had a growing pool of blood on the right leg of his britches. His leg buckled a bit as he stepped, he caught himself on the wagon before he fell.

"They got my leg," he said. In all the excitement he didn't feel it, but now it was painful. Silas got down and helped Cody back on the wagon. He then tied Cody's horse to the wagon. Cody had torn his britches to find that a bullet had grazed his leg deep. He tied a kerchief around the wounded leg and sat quietly for the ride home.

Chapter 10

Every morning Zeke would help bring water from the creek and put out some grain before taking the shovel and heading off. Every evening he would come back dirty and covered with sweat. He would be so tired after helping water the cattle in the evening that he would eat and fall asleep quickly. It was the fifth day after they got back from the trading post that he rode back in the early afternoon, gleaming with pride. He found Silas who had been secretly practicing his quick draw.

"Water!" Zeke announced, "under rock, water."

Silas called Cody and Fred over and they followed Zeke out to the dry spring. Except now it wasn't dry. Zeke had dug until he got water. He was one determined man. Fred looked close to tears and the pond slowly filled up, the parched ground turning soft again. He walked over to Zeke and thanked him for helping save his family. Zeke just gave him a big grin and turned his horse back around.

"Where are you going?" Silas asked.

"Cows thirsty," responded the big man as he rode off. The three men laughed and followed him. It was not long before they had moved the cattle closer to the water. They lapped up the water almost as fast as it came out of the spring.

In a few days the pond had filled up. There were even signs that grass would be coming up soon. Silas had never really seen drought and was amazed at how a little water brought everything to life. He was sitting on a fence rail thinking about all this when he felt someone behind him. He turned around and saw Mary standing there with a small parcel held carefully in her hands.

"Ma baked a pie," Mary said, offering the parcel. She had put a cloth over it to keep it warm. "She says I should give it to you boys to thank you."

Silas jumped off the fence and took the pie from Mary. Her eyes were the same color as Emily's but there wasn't the same joy in them. Silas thanked her and took the pie.

"Pa says the pond is filled up," Mary continued.

"That's right," said Silas. "Zeke dug the spring out."

"That must have been hard work," Mary said.

"He's a man that doesn't mind hard work," Silas said.

"I think I'm gonna go take a look at that pond," Mary said offhandedly, "enjoy the pie." Mary climbed over the fence, she did it in a manner that wasn't very ladylike, while Emily was no stranger to climbing or being with animals, she always struck Silas as being very feminine about it all. He watched Mary walk off for a second and then remembered the pie.

The five men each took their share of pie and dug in. It was a crabapple pie, which was tart, but Susan did a great job of sweetening it with honey and it tasted perfect. Silas was hoping for another piece when he heard a yell from by the pond. Before anyone could respond he had jumped on his horse and rode it bareback holding onto the horse's mane. It took a minute to get there at full gallop. When he got there, he saw Mary on the ground and a strange man on top of her. He was holding her down with one hand and the other was fighting to lift her skirts. Silas jumped off the horse and grabbed him.

"Who are you?" the man insisted.

"That doesn't matter," Silas said, "what the devil do you think you're doing."

"Mary and I are betrothed," said the man. Silas looked at him, he was probably seventeen or eighteen.

"Maybe you are, maybe you aren't," Silas said, "but you never should treat a woman like that." Mary was slowly getting off the ground, her hands brushing her skirts back down.

"This is Jake Slade," Mary said quietly, "his Pa told my Pa I have to marry him or else." Silas stared at Jake, he was taller than Silas, and much heavier looking. Silas had the muscular build of someone who has worked hard every day of his life. Jake looked soft, he was working on a double chin to rival his father. His eyes were narrow and mean, Silas felt sorry for any woman that married this man.

"I think you should leave," Silas said.

"I'm not leaving until I get a kiss," he said, looking at Mary. Mary took a step away, a frightened look on her face.

"She doesn't look like she wants a kiss," Silas said, "I think you should just go on your way." Silas took a step towards Jake who stepped back. He had an irritating smirk on his face, but it was starting to waver.

"She's just a girl," Jake's voice quivered a little, but the smirk stayed, "who cares what she wants."

"I care," Silas said, another step forward, "now leave before I make you leave." This time Jake stepped forward and punched Silas in the face. Silas took the punch straight on the mouth and didn't move back. He could taste blood; he squared up and threw a punch at Jake.

Jake staggered back but managed to keep his feet under him. Silas stepped in as Jake tried to throw another punch, it glanced off his cheek bone, Silas was so riled up he barely felt it. Silas punched low into the gut, and Jake coughed as the air was knocked out of him. Silas then came up with a punch square on Jake's jaw. Jake fell back into the pond behind him.

Jake came up sputtering and stepped out of the pond. He stepped toward Silas again; Silas was a little surprised he hadn't quit. Jake tried to punch Silas in the gut, but Silas saw it coming and tightened his muscles. The punch hurt, but Silas stood straight and looked at Jake. He then threw a haymaker and connected square on Jake's jaw. There was a sickening thud and Jake crumpled forward to the ground. He was out.

Silas heard some clapping and cheering behind him and saw Curly, Cody, Tobais and Zeke on their horses clapping and hollering. "Where were you guys?" Silas asked.

"You looked like you had things taken care of," Cody said with a smile.

"Silas, you're bleeding!" Mary said with concern, walking over to him. Silas knew that the first punch drew some blood, he looked down and his shirt was covered in blood. He felt his lips and found the tender spot where the lip had split. He walked over to the pond and splashed some water on his face. The cool water slowed any bleeding down.

"So, what do we do with this poor guy?" Tobias asked, pointing at Jake's limp body, laying on the ground. Silas looked at him, he was breathing, but still out cold.

"We should probably take him somewhere safe," Cody said, "don't really want him at our camp though."

"He lives about three miles north of here," Mary said quietly. Jake's horse was standing nearby drinking peacefully like nothing had happened. Cody dismounted and grabbed the reins of Jake's horse.

"We can't just put him on the horse and send them home," he said thoughtfully, "he might fall off. I guess someone should deliver him home." The five men all looked around at each other, nobody wanting the job.

"His Pa's going to be mad," Mary finally said, looking at her attacker on the ground. She had been truly frightened when he rode up on her while she was looking at the pond. He didn't really say much before throwing her to the ground and kissing her. She screamed and he slapped her before trying to touch her. She had been so relieved when Silas showed up and stopped him. She still could feel his hot breath on her as she tried to fight him.

"Should be mad at him," Silas said, thinking of the scene he saw as he arrived. "That boy has problems."

Cody chuckled at Silas calling someone older a "boy," and said, "yeah, he can't take a punch."

"We still need to figure out what to do with him," Silas was ready to be done with this whole situation.

"Slade doesn't seem a reasonable man," Cody said, "it's likely best we all go. Silas you can go get cleaned up."

"I'm ok," Silas responded, "I'll come too. Explain the whole thing."

"He won't listen," Mary said. Jake started to stir and Silas hoped he would wake up and solve the problem by heading home on his own. He sat up suddenly and looked around at all the men standing around him. Silas breathed a sigh of relief.

Jake stood up and looked at them, he saw Cody holding his horse and yelled "horse thief!"

"I'm holding your horse," Cody said with a smile, "while you took a little nap." Jake scowled at Cody. He put a hand on his gun about to draw when a big hand came from behind him and clamped his hand to his side. Zeke spun him around and looked down at him.

"Be good," Zeke said gently. Jake quickly used his free hand to punch Zeke in the stomach, which had no effect on the big man. Cody however was nearly bent double laughing. This feisty kid was real entertainment. Zeke clamped his other hand to his side and effortlessly picked him up and placed him roughly on his horse's back. "Be good!" Zeke said sternly. Jake finally relaxed his muscles, unable to escape Zeke's grip.

"I'm still thinking we should escort the lad home," Cody said, "make sure he makes no more trouble for us."

"Sounds good," Tobias said, "I'll come too." Curly wanted to go along, he was a little sore he had missed the last fight. He wasn't missing this one. Zeke was determined to keep this boy behaving and decided to come too.

Silas looked at the group and over at Mary. Poor Mary was not amused by any of this, and why would she be? Silas noticed for the first time that her dress was torn at her shoulder, and some pale skin was showing through. He also had a red handprint on her face where Jake had slapped her. Silas looked over at his friends.

"I think I'll take Mary home," he said quietly, "she shouldn't be alone." Cody looked at the girl and the smile faded. He had forgotten what had started this whole thing and walked over to Mary.

"Mary," he said, removing his hat, "I'm terribly sorry for what happened here. We will make sure his Pa knows what he did here. You've no need to bother thinking about it."

"His Pa won't care," she said, "he'll just laugh."

"That's likely true," Cody said, "but I'll make sure they know that you're my kin. Any man touches you again there'll be hell to pay." Mary looked at Cody with tears in her eyes and wrapped her arms around him. Silas brought his pony over, there was no saddle since he left too fast to saddle her. Mary had walked over and had no horse.

"Zeke, can you help her onto my horse please?" Silas asked. Zeke pointed at Jake and reminded him to behave before walking over and gently lifting Mary onto Silas' pony. He smiled at her and patted her knee.

Silas borrowed a rope from Cody and used it to lead the pony off. He could hear Jake cussing out the men and telling them he could go home by himself. They just followed behind him, laughing and joking as they went.

The ride back to the adobe cabin was quick, Mary was never a talkative person, but right now she seemed to be so deep inside herself that she didn't barely say or do anything. When they arrived, Susan was just coming out of the cabin. She saw the two and dropped the bucket she was carrying and rushed over to them.

"What happened?" Susan asked, taking in the blood on Silas' shirt and Mary's torn dress.

"Jake Slade attacked her ma'am," Silas said, helping Mary off the pony. "I'm afraid she's a bit shook up."

"That boy is a menace," Susan said with a scowl. "You are covered in blood son, are you ok?"

"I'm fine," Silas said. Mary was leaning onto him for support. "I think we should get her inside." Susan helped Silas take Mary inside. Once inside they took Mary to her bed behind the hanging quilt. Mary lay down and turned to face the wall.

"You go sit down," Susan ordered Silas, "after I get her settled, I'm going to want to know what all happened." Silas sat down in a chair while Susan took a minute helping get Mary cleaned up. He felt a little awkward hearing them move around. Susan stepped out after a minute with Mary's torn dress in her hands. Silas could just see Mary's eyes as she stared out from behind the quilt.

"What on earth happened out there," Susan said sitting in the other chair. Silas told her the whole story, from him finding Jake on top of Mary to the men escorting Jake home. Susan just sat there with a pained expression on her face. When he was done, she hung her head for a minute. Silas wasn't sure if she was crying but felt a little uncomfortable and unsure what to do.

"I hate that man," Susan said quietly. She looked up with wet eyes and once more noticed the state of Silas clothes. "My word!" she exclaimed, "I'm sorry, I've been making you sit here in that state."

"Ma'am, it's really fine," Silas said.

"No, you came to my daughter's rescue, and I leave you like this." Susan stood up and went over to her side of the cabin. She came back with a shirt. "Now you change into one of my husband's shirts and I'll wash that one for you." Silas looked at the shirt, it would swallow him whole. Fred wasn't a big man but was a lot taller than Silas.

"Thank you," Silas said with a smile, "I have more shirts in my saddle bag."

"Well take that one off and leave it here," Susan insisted, "I'm going to wash it for you." Silas started to refuse, but Susan had a look on her face that made him change his mind. He quietly removed his shirt and thanked Susan for taking care of it. On his way out he noticed that Mary was sitting up a little to watch him walk out the door.

Chapter 11

Silas was putting on his fresh shirt when the others returned from escorting Jake Slade home. He didn't realize he had been in the cabin so long. Curly was the first to dismount and as he unsaddled and brushed his horse he told Silas the whole story.

Jake had spent the whole trip cussing them and telling them to leave. He even kicked out at any rider that got too close. When they arrived at the Slade ranch, he yelled out for help, telling everyone he was being attacked by bandits. Several men came running, ready to fight. When Burton Slade came out of the house, Jake jumped off his horse and ran to him blubbering. Burton recognized Cody and walked over to him about ready to fight. Cody explained that they were just escorting his son home after a fight. Cody calmly explained that he had been knocked out and they wanted to make sure he made it home safely.

When Burton had asked how he got knocked out, they explained that someone was defending the honor of a young lady. Burton refused to believe that his boy could be guilty of anything of the sort, Cody got off his horse and faced him down man to man. In recounting the story, Curly got real serious at this point.

"Silas," Curly said, "I'm Cody's friend and am glad to be that. I tell you I would hate to face off with him like that. My blood ran cold the way he told him that messing with his kin was asking for a slow death."

After hearing all this, Silas walked out among his cattle. He needed a moment to decompress; it had been a long day. The sun was setting, and he stood in the field and watched the beautiful colors appear in the sky. Silas had never understood why the sky lit up like that but was always glad when it did. Silas sensed someone behind him and turned to see Mary standing behind him. She was quietly watching him. The dress she was wearing was obviously older, and her ankles were showing. He looked away and into her eyes. She smiled at him and stepped a little closer.

"I want to thank you for rescuing me today," she said softly.

"Of course," Silas says shyly, "it was the right thing to do." She looked at his lip and brought her hand close to it.

"Does it hurt much?" she asked.

"Hardly notice it," Silas said, he wasn't trying to be tough, that was the truth. Mary brought her hand back down and moved a little closer. She was right in front of him, looking up into his eyes. He looked back at her. His eyes wandered to her lips. She looked like she wanted to be kissed. He could kiss her, here with this beautiful sunset. She was beautiful, so much like Emily.

He looked back toward the sunset and turned a little. He cared for Emily, he missed Emily. He would enjoy kissing Mary, and he was sure she wanted that too. However, it wouldn't be right. He turned back to look at Mary again.

"Mary," his voice cracked, "I think you are a wonderful person. I really could kiss you right now," she smiled, "but I have to tell you I can't." Mary frowned so Silas continued, "your cousin Emily took care of me when I was shot, we spent a lot of time together."

"And you're in love with her." Mary finished the thought.

"I think so," said Silas. Love was a complicated thing, but he did know he always thought about her. Mary backed away and smiled at Silas.

"She's lucky," Mary said, "I hope to meet her someday, what's she like?" Silas spent the next several minutes telling Mary all about a cousin she didn't know. She listened carefully and smiled when he was done. "You are definitely in love," she concluded. Silas escorted Mary back to the cabin, and Tobias saw them and smiled. After Mary went inside Tobias went over and nudged Silas.

"How are things?" he asked with a knowing smile.

"Fine," Silas said, walking toward the campfire. Susan had sent out an amazing spread of cornbread, roast game hen with carrots, fried potatoes, and fresh cider. They even got a molasses cake to eat. They men had a great time eating and joking around. It had been a rough day for Silas and this time with friends was the perfect way to end the day.

As he drifted off to sleep, Silas kept thinking about Emily. Those few weeks recovering from a bullet wound were made sweet by a daily visit from Emily. She would come and sit by his bed and tell him all that was going on at the ranch. Her Pa's horse had also been shot in the shoulder around the same time so she would tease him for being a worse patient than the horse. He drifted off to sleep with a big smile on his face.

Silas woke with a start. He had heard something and wasn't the only one. Cody and Tobias already had their boots and gun belts on. Curly was moving around, and Zeke was nowhere to be seen.

"What is it?" Silas asked Cody.

"Riders coming," Cody answered. "We can't figure how many. Zeke went out scouting, he heard something first and woke me up before heading out. Silas got up and put his boots on; he was buckling his gun belt when Zeke walked up to them.

"Too many," Zeke said. Cody gave Tobias a worried look.

"We need to wake up the family," Cody said, "let them know trouble might be coming."

"Yes. Trouble." Zeke was already going over to the cabin. As Zeke knocked on the door, Silas and Curly joined the other two men looking out towards the definite sound of many horses.

"Silas," Cody said looking around, "you and Curly go to the house with Zeke. Tobias and I will fight from out here." The cabin only had three windows, so the plan made some sense. Only three people could fire out anyway. Silas waved at Curly to come with him. "We'll be by the corral," Cody hissed at them, "try not to shoot us." Silas couldn't see his face in the dark but knew he was smiling. The man had a dark sense of humor.

When they got to the cabin, the door was open and Fred was standing there in a nightshirt. Zeke was already putting the table on its side in front of the fire. It would give the women something to hide behind and prevent any shadows from the fireplace giving their position. For someone touched in the head, Zeke was good in a crisis. They rushed in and latched the door behind them. Silas and Curly entered the cabin and looked around. Susan and Mary were in their nightgowns and looked frightened. Mary looked relieved to see her hero enter the cabin and rushed over to him.

"What's going on?" Mary asked Silas, hugging his arm close.

"Riders," he said, trying to sound like it was nothing. "We just wanted to be ready in case it's Slade's men."

"Of course it's Slade's men," Susan said angrily, "who else would it be?" Fred went over and put an arm around his wife. She buried her head in his shoulder and started to cry. Silas indicated to Mary to go to her Ma. Mary took her Ma and the two sat down behind the table. Fred rushed to get britches and boots on. He was strapping his gun on when they heard the voice of Slade coming from outside.

"Hello Locke!" Slade yelled, "Come out, I want to talk to you."

"I can talk from here," Fred yelled out. Silas went to the window, keeping low, and looked out. He could see about fifteen men out there, sitting on their horses. The Slade's were easy to spot, both bigger than all the men around them. Silas couldn't help but think only a fool would show up like this when they are an easy target, even in the dark.

"I want the boy that beat up my son," Slade continued, "I need to teach him a lesson."

"You can't have him," Fred said, "from what I hear your son attacked my girl."

"You heard wrong," Slade yelled back, "my boy was beaten by five men."

"Your boy was beaten by another boy half his size and a foot shorter than him," Silas yelled. "And I didn't even have to try."

"Who said that!" yelled Slade.

"Short Hand Trent," Silas yelled out smiling, might as well accept the name. "You remember me don't you? Shot two of your men last time we met." Curly laughed, but Fred scowled at him.

"Don't anger him," Fred hissed at him.

"He's already mad," said Curly. "I swear that man was born with a chip on his shoulder."

"That's true," said a feminine voice from behind the table. Silas never figured out who said that because the shooting started. Slade's men started shooting at the house and glass flew everywhere. Silas peeked out and noticed that both Slade's had left, so maybe they weren't as foolish. He shot at one of the men and got back down again. Curly and Fred were shooting sporadically as well. Zeke was over by the fireplace with a knife in his hand. Silas didn't have time to figure out what he was doing.

Silas found an angle where he could see and aimed at one of the men. He watched his target drop his weapon and grab his leg. Silas decided he really needed to work on his aim instead of his draw. He fired again and saw the next man fall. They were moving around more now, so he wasn't likely to find an easy target again. He rushed over to the table and joined the women, who were hunkered down low. He figured to take a stand here if the men out there made it in. He put a hand on Mary's back, and she turned to look at him. He smiled confidently, even though he didn't feel it.

Curly swore from his vantage point. "Torches!" he cried out. Silas crawled back to his window and looked out again. The shooting had slowed, and Silas could see the orange glow of torches in the riders' hands.

"They're going to burn the place!" Fred shouted. Silas watched as one of the riders with a torch fell from his horse. Cody and Tobias were still out there, maybe they could still stop them from burning the house down around them. Another rider fell, Silas was hopeful, carrying torches did make the riders an easier target. He took aim and shot another one.

Curly yelled and Silas looked back to see he was on fire; a torch had come in his window and landed too close to him. Zeke grabbed one of the hanging quilts and wrapped Curly up tight. The flames were out, but Curly was whimpering. The bed under the window had caught fire, and Zeke tried fighting it. It was too late, more torches were flying in. All was lost. Silas went over to Mary and wrapped his arms around her. Perhaps his body could protect her from the flames. He looked over and watched Fred do the same with Susan. Silas mind went back to the day his father died, he had been shot and left for dead. He remembered lying there, when he watched his father take his last breath. His final word was "Martha," the name of Silas' Ma.

Silas whispered to Mary that no matter what happened to let him protect her. He wished her a happy life. He could hear her sob and prepared himself for death. His thoughts were interrupted by someone calling his name. Zeke was calling them over to where he had been doing something with his knife. He had already dragged Curly over, still wrapped in the quilt.

Zeke had been digging through the clay wall with his knife. "That will take forever," Fred said, "that wall's at least a foot thick." Zeke smiled and threw all his weight at the wall. Cracks started to form in the wall. He threw himself at it again and the wall gave way and a small opening appeared. Fresh air rushed in feeding the flames.

"Back door," Zeke said, the teeth of his smile shining through the soot that was covering his face.

"Zeke," Silas said, "you're a good brother!" Fred and Silas helped the women out through the opening. They were quiet as they could be, so they didn't attract any attention. Zeke followed, dragging Curly. They stayed low and moved away from the cabin. The fire was in the walls now and the roof was ablaze. They rushed to the pond where Zeke used the quilt to put cool water on Curly's burns.

Silas crawled back to the corral and found Cody and Tobias, watching the cabin burn in silence. Slade and his men were riding around cheering jubilantly. Silas crawled up bedside them and whispered, "glad I'm not in there." Cody and Tobias jumped and looked over at Silas.

"Where did you come from?" Cody asked.

"The pond," Silas said, "everyone's there, but Curly's hurt." The three snuck over to the pond where Tobias looked at Curly's wounds in the moonlight. He told Curly it wasn't bad but would hurt until he had a chance to get some medicinal plants in the morning.

The group sat by the pond feeling dejected. Silas had a protective arm around Mary, feeling like this was all his fault. Maybe he should have just stopped Jake and made him leave. He kept going over the day trying to think what he could have done differently. He had been cocky, and they had mocked the Slade family. They shouldn't have, now their actions left this family without a home. He looked over at Mary and saw that somehow; she was fast asleep.

Chapter 12

When the sun came up, they were all still by the pond. Cody, Silas and the Locke family walked over to where the Cabin once stood. Some of the adobe walls had survived, but there was little that could be salvaged. Silas was also discouraged to see that the gate to the corral was lying flat on the ground, and all his cattle were gone. Stolen.

"What now?" Fred asked, kicking at the gate.

"I'm going to kill Slade and get my herd back," Silas said quietly.

"Isn't this how we met?" Cody said with a sad smile.

"Not many men have had all their cattle stolen twice," Silas said sadly.

"Makes you special," Cody said, putting an arm around Silas' shoulder. Silas looked at him incredulously.

"Seriously" Silas said, "we need a plan."

"Fred and I were talking last night about taking the women to safety in Albuquerque, it will take three days by wagon," Cody explained. "Maybe we all go. We need more supplies, anyway."

"I guess I don't have anything here," Silas said with resignation.

The ride to Albuquerque was a quiet one, even the evenings at camp were quiet. The plants that Tobias had used on Curly's burns worked quickly, but he was too sore for storytelling. It was a sad looking group that entered Albuquerque. The ladies had not dressed before leaving the cabin, Susan was wearing Cody's coat and Mary had Silas' coat.

Silas pulled ten dollars from his boot and gave it to Susan so that she could buy some clothes first thing. They went to a small hotel, since money was getting tight. After getting settled they all met in the hotel's saloon and grabbed some food. Cody walked over to a boy standing by the door. He said something to the boy and handed him a dime before joining the table. Silas gave him a look, and he just smiled.

The food was good, and their spirits were starting to lighten. They might have lost everything, but they were alive. Silas was certain that they would get his cattle back, but he still hadn't come up with a decent plan. Cody was acting like he had a plan but wasn't talking. As they were finishing their meal Tobias, who was facing the door stopped eating and just stared. Silas wondered what was going on and turned around to see Emily. She was standing at the entrance to the room, looking around. When she saw him, her face lit up and she rushed over to him. Before he could ask how she got here, Silas noticed she was with her Ma and Pa. He wanted to wrap his arms around her but made do with a long handshake.

"Surprise!" exclaimed Cody. Fred stood up and looked at Henry Locke, his cousin. They hadn't seen each other for decades.

"What are you doing here?" Fred asked the question everyone, except Cody, was wondering.

"We got a letter a while back from Cody," Henry explained, "telling us he had met up with kinfolk in trouble. You saved me from a few scrapes back in the day Fred. I couldn't leave you without help. I left Jesse in charge of the ranch and came running"

"How is Jesse?" Silas asked.

"He's mending nicely," Emily said with a smile, "the doctor said Kent did the right thing from the start."

They scrounged up more chairs so everyone could sit. Silas had to let go of Emily but kept looking over at her. She kept stealing glances as well. After giving Henry and Jane a rundown on the troubles, Henry leaned back in his chair. He took out a tobacco pouch and started rolling a cigarette. Cody smiled, he was making plans.

"First things, first," Henry turned to Zeke and Curly, "I know my boy hired you on the trail to replace Jesse and poor James Smith. I'll keep you on, but I don't pay people to fight my battles. You don't want to fight; you don't have to."

Curly smiled and said, "I'm not giving up a chance to see the Appalachian Kid at work."

"I'm the Appalachian Old Man now," Henry quipped, "I may not work like you want me to." He turned to Zeke, "what about you, young man."

Zeke furrowed his brow; he was thinking hard about what Henry had said. Finally, Zeke said, "Silas has no Pa." This took Henry by surprise; he cocked his head a little and looked around the table.

"That means he's my brother, because he's got no Pa," Silas explained, "brothers always stick together." Zeke nodded vigorously so Henry knew that was an accurate translation.

"Well Silas I'm glad to meet your kin," Henry said with a wink. "Next, I'm a firm believer in the law." Silas knew this was true; he had seen Henry wait patiently for the law to sort things out. It didn't always work, but that didn't change his thinking.

"The marshal!" Cody exclaimed, "Bill Wallace. He might be able to help."

"We can try to get in touch with him," Henry added. "Finally, we need to go back out there and make sure Slade knows he can't take things from the Locke's without consequences." This was something Silas wanted to hear. "We have two rooms over at the Highland Hotel. I suggest that tomorrow the ladies all move over there and we head back."

Silas loved how Henry took control and made some plans. He was not as happy about leaving Emily behind again. He looked over at her, her golden hair was up in a bun, and she was dressed for being in town with a satin dress the color of the sky. He couldn't get over how wonderful it was to be sitting next to her.

"Cody, Fred and I will go see if we can find the marshal," Henry added, "Silas, can you help Jane and Emily back to the hotel?" Silas agreed wholeheartedly. "Maybe take Susan and Mary as well. The four ladies can get to know each other while we get things ready." This wasn't as good for Silas.

They all got up to head out. Henry gave Tobias and Curly the money to buy the dry goods and ammunition they might need. Zeke went with them to help with some of the lifting. Silas left with the women, leading them back to the Highland.

The Highland impressed Susan and Mary, they loved the fancy dining room. They went in and Jane ordered tea for everyone. They sat and talked for a while, the women doing most of the talking, getting to know kin they had never met. Silas found it interesting that they were so willing to go from being perfect strangers to relatives. They told stories and commiserated on the problems of being a rancher's wife. Silas sat quietly and listened, he was enjoying being in Emily's presence. They would occasionally catch each other's eyes and smile. After a while Jane caught this and smiled.

"Silas," she said, "we're completely ignoring you. How have you been?"

"Fine ma'am," Silas said.

"Silas stayed with us for a while," Jane said with a smile "he became like family." Silas saw Emily's smile.

"Yes, he mentioned that he enjoyed his time with you," Mary said with a knowing smile. Silas gave her a look, and she smiled kindly. He didn't sense that she was jealous. "Now that I've met you all, I can see why." Emily gave Silas a funny look, and he looked away.

Jane was watching all of this and made a mental note to talk things over with Emily and Henry. She quickly changed the topic, and they started to make plans for their time in Albuquerque.

Henry had convinced Marshal Wallace to join them, and he rode up as Silas was saddling his horse for the ride back. "Short Hand Trent, is it?" Wallace asked as he rode up.

"I guess that's me now," Silas responded. The marshal laughed as Silas got on his horse. They joined the others around the wagon and started their journey back. It was comforting on the journey back to have the weight of the law behind them. Wallace was certain that once the judge heard about the attack on Mary and the intentional burning of a house they knew was occupied both father and son Slade would end up in prison.

When they arrived at the burned-out adobe cabin and empty corral, they noticed a bunch of flowers laying by the door to the cabin. They were wildflowers and had obviously been intentionally picked and placed there. It was late afternoon, and they were tired from the trail, so they didn't think on it for long. They just set up camp and discussed plans for the next day.

The marshal's plan was to ride out and arrest Slade the next day. They had to surprise him since Slade was surrounded by hired guns. He joked that if four men he thought were dead showing up didn't surprise him, nothing would. The thought of how he might react amused them.

Everyone quietened down and sat back to enjoy the evening. Each one wondering what the next day would bring. Silas got to thinking about Emily, he was sure she felt the same as he did. He moved over to Henry and asked him to talk. They moved away from the campfire.

"Sir," Silas started, "I would like to speak with you about your daughter." Jane had warned Henry this was coming but he gave Silas a stern look and stood quietly. "Well sir," Silas continued, "I have strong feelings for her, and I think she might feel the same. I'm looking for permission to court her"

"You have an odd sense of timing son," Henry said sternly.

"Well sir," Silas said with a sly grin, "there might be fighting tomorrow, one of us might be killed. I'd die happy knowing I might have married Emily if I lived." Henry had a hard time keeping a straight face.

"You have been spending too much time with Cody," Henry said, "his bad humor is rubbing off on you. What are your plans?"

"Not sure yet," Silas said honestly, "I have to get my cattle home, and get myself ready to take care of a family. I will come back when I'm ready and if she'll have me, I will want to marry her."

"That's a good plan," Henry said, "I will say you are welcome to come calling when you are ready. If you want to start courting here, now that's up to the two of you. I won't stop you."

The two men walked back to the camp and Tobias was standing, looking towards the burnt-out cabin. "There's a shadow by the cabin," he whispered, "I swear I saw someone moving over there." The men all turned their heads to look over to the cabin. Silas was certain he saw something too and started to move closer to the cabin. He palmed his colt and quietly cocked it. Silas made a wide arch around the cabin and could see Tobias was going around the other side. As he got to the far side of the cabin, he could see a stout figure crouched behind it. Silas was sure it was Jake Slade. He moved over to Tobias and touched his shoulder.

"Slade!" he shouted, the figure jumped and took off running, right towards them. As he got closer, they could see the round face of Jake Slade, already a bit winded from the run. Tobias stood up and grabbed the young man's shoulders and stopped his escape. They dragged him back to the camp; he let his distress be well known. When they got to the camp he was trying to kick at Tobias and struggling to be let free.

"Calm down, lad, they aren't going to kill you," Wallace said with a booming voice. The sound of authority made Jake calm down a little as he looked around the camp. He was surprised to see men he had seen burn to death standing in front of him.

"You're supposed to be dead," he said to Fred.

"I think that sounds like a confession," said Henry. Jake sank back into Tobias, a little unsure of what was going on.

"Does this mean Mary's still alive?" Jake said hopefully, "where is she?"

"Safe," Silas said, stepping into the light of the fire so Jake could see him. Jake stiffened, his facial expression changed to one of pure hatred. Henry stepped forward, and Jake looked over at him.

"What's your name?" Henry asked.

"Jake Slade," said the boy, "my father is Burton Slade."

"That name means nothing to me," Henry said. Jake's face fell; he was used to his family name bringing fear to people. He didn't think that some people might never have heard of him. "Your name I've heard. You're the one that attacked my cousin." Jake's lower lip started to quiver.

"I didn't. She's my gal," Jake said in his defense. Henry looked back at Fred, who stepped forward.

"You have no right to claim that" Fred said, "she's my daughter and I never gave you permission to court." Jake glared at him; it was his father that gave the permission around here.

"So," the marshal said, stepping forward, his badge flashing in the light of the fire, "based on your confession of trying to kill Mary Locke and the testimony of these witnesses that you assaulted Miss Locke earlier that day, I am placing you under arrest." Wallace pulled out some handcuffs and placed them on Jake's wrists.

Jake just stood there dumbfounded, he had been brought up thinking he was above the law. The marshal in Albuquerque was the closest law, so Slade was able to run the place like he was the law. Wallace directed Jake to sit by the fire. They gave him a blanket, and he hunkered down, looking dejected.

Zeke got up and went for a walk. He came back a minute later leading a horse, Jake's presumably. Zeke took the saddle and bridle off the horse and gave it a careful brush down and let it loose in the corral.

Chapter 13

The Silas house lay on a slight plateau overlooking the huge valley. Since it would be impossible to sneak up on the house, Marshal Wallace rode in first with his badge showing. He rode in alone, the rest hiding the shadows of the hills. Afraid that Jake would give them away, they muzzled him.

As the marshal got up to the house there was a fair bit of concern among the men. Many were wanted men and immediately found something to keep them occupied. Wallace went up to the house and knocked on the door. A Mexican woman opened the door a crack and looked out.

"Si?" asked the woman.

"I'm looking for Burton Slade," the marshal said.

"Who is?" asked the woman.

"I'm US Marshal Bill Wallace; I'm here with news about his son." The door slammed open, and Wallace saw a large man standing where the door had blocked him from view. The Mexican woman stepped back. The big man said something in Spanish and the woman rushed off.

"I'm Slade," the big man said, "what's happened to my boy?"

"He's been arrested for assault with attempt to ravish and attempted murder," the marshal said, "we have him over yonder. I'm here to arrest you as well." Slade stepped back, he had been worried about his son since he realized Jake hadn't been home all night. Things were getting worse. There was a moment he thought about fighting, his rifle was mounted on the wall next to the door, he looked at it. It was loaded and ready to go.

Wallace saw his eyes shift to his gun. "Don't even think about it," he said, "I have deputies waiting just over yonder with your son. Anyone shoots at me, and they will rain holy hell on you. You wouldn't last the day." Slade sighed and raised his hands. Wallace drew his gun and walked him out to his horse, hands raised so everyone could see who was in charge now.

At the horse, Wallace made a show of handcuffing Slade and then called one of the few men who weren't hiding over. When the man got closer, Wallace asked for Slade's horse to be saddled and brought to him. When the horse came out Wallace helped Slade up on his horse and mounted his own.

As they rode out, they were being watched by men who dreaded coming against the lawman that could catch them. Wallace rode out, his head held high. He figured he could beat this charge, he left no witnesses, and his men were too loyal to talk. They rode out to the edge of the valley.

Sitting on their horses were all the men Slade thought he had killed. His jaw dropped when he saw them. Fred Locke smiling like a fool, that dumb kid, the wannabe gunfighter and the one with the mouth, his smile made Slade want to punch him. With the two Slade's arrested, the group left to head back to Albuquerque.

Burton was still riding with arrogant confidence, after getting over the initial shock, he sat up and glared at everyone. He was now quietly riding next to his son. Silas had heard him mutter quietly to Jake but couldn't make out the words.

They got to a valley where the hills rolled high over them. They had been riding for several hours and had fallen into an order of sorts. Wallace led the group with Cody beside

90

him. Tobias and Curly rode off to the side a little, with their prisoners between them. Henry was riding next to Silas and Zeke was behind the whole group. Silas looked over at Slade and realized he was looking up in the hills. Silas followed his gaze up the hill and saw movement. He dismissed it at first to be an animal, but then he saw more movement that was human.

"Ambush!" he shouted, spurring his horse onward and grabbing his rifle. Everyone took off riding hard, both prisoners finding it difficult to hold on with their hands clasped in front of them. As soon as they sped up the firing started from the hills. They could see the hills forming a natural bottleneck in front of them.

"That's where they'll try to cut us off," Henry yelled pointing at the bottleneck, "Cody. Silas, you try to lead them through, Kent with me!" Tobias and Henry broke off from the group, riding wide and into the hills on either side. Silas and Cody joined Wallace at the front while Curly and Zeke rode the flanks of the prisoners. Silas heard Zeke grunt and turned and saw he was holding his left shoulder. He had been hit but hadn't slowed down. As they got closer to the bottleneck Silas and Cody spurred their horses. They put the rifles away and grabbed their pistols. They could see some riders ahead with rifles aimed at them. There were too many of them, Silas and Cody turned at the last minute, slowing down and coming together to regroup as the rest of their group caught up.

From the hills a loud noise echoed, it was a half yell, half screech. It was answered by an undulating cry that echoed. Cody laughed, "it's Pa and Kent," he explained to Silas. The riders blocking the way out looked up into the hills confused.

"That's a Paiute war cry!" Wallace exclaimed, "we will all be kilt."

Cody looked at him and was inspired with a plan. He started to ride around looking panicked, shooting randomly into the hills. The others in the group just stopped, looking confused.

"There's one over there!" Cody yelled shooting "Paiute warrior for sure!"

Silas realized what he was doing and shouted, "I see ten riding in coming from behind!" They rode straight at the ambush yelling about Paiute warriors. The men didn't know what to think when the cry echoed again. When two men suddenly lurched forward, dead on their horses. The riders turned and hightailed it out of there. After they were gone, the men stayed alert until Henry and Tobias rode out of the hills. Henry slapped Cody on the shoulder, proud of his son for coming up with a plan.

Chapter 14

Silas sat by the burnt-out cabin, looking at the cattle he had collected from Slade's ranch. The sun was rising behind him, giving them an ethereal glow. He was itching to head out, but the marshal had asked him to return to Albuquerque to testify against Jake Slade. The circuit judge was due to be in town in a couple of days, so Silas would head back for trial after breakfast.

The men had all been helping the Locke family build a new house a little closer to the pond. It was bigger, three rooms, so Mary could have a private space. It took almost a month, and the house was almost finished. The women had come to supervise the finishing touches to the house, Silas and Cody had combined the remaining amount of their reward money to help with the furnishings.

Zeke had been wounded during the ambush; a bullet had entered his shoulder. The women had nursed him back to health and he came with them to see the house next to the pond. His face lit up when they told him they decided to name the pond 'Zeke's Pond.'

As Silas got up from where he was sitting, he saw Emily walking from the new house. He smiled as she approached and put out his hand, she took it and looked into his eyes.

"Pa says you'll be heading out after the trial" Emily said sadly.

"I have to finish the drive," Silas said, "I'm so close to home I can taste it." Emily smiled, she leaned in and kissed him on the cheek.

"I hope to see it someday," she said quietly.

"That is the plan," Silas said, "once I get settled, I'm coming calling."

"I will hold you to that Silas Trent." She let go of his hands and rushed off towards to saddle her own horse. They had found a few moments together, and Silas was more certain than ever that Emily was the girl for him.

The group of them that would be testifying were heading out. Henry and Zeke would stay with the cattle and continue a few finishing touches on the house. They were a happy group to be heading back to see the big city one more time before heading off. Henry's family had tickets to ride the train home, and Silas and the team would drive the cattle home. After the trial.

They were staying at the Highland hotel, and Silas couldn't help but think Zeke would be happy he stayed with the cows. After they got settled, they were visited by the territorial district attorney. He was a sour looking man, with grey hair and a well-tailored suit. He introduced himself as Elias Maddox. Maddox spent the next half an hour discussing procedure and some questions they might ask.

Since Silas was the only one to witness the attempted rape of Mary, he was asked to testify in both trials. The first trial would be for Jake, because there were only three people who could give witness, the trial would be short. The day after the attempted murder trial would start. The district attorney felt they would both be sent to jail for a long time.

When the time came for his testimony, Silas entered the courtroom. To him it looked like a big hall with a desk at the front. Twelve men, the Jury the attorney called them, sat looking at Silas as he entered. He went to the chair they told him to sit in. A deputy made him swear to tell the truth and then the questions started.

They had him tell his side of the story without too many problems. Then this other man stood up, Silas knew he was Jake's lawyer and started to ask some questions.

"What made you think my client was assaulting Miss Locke," he asked.

"He was on top of her," Silas said simply.

"Could you not have just come up on a couple in a romantic embrace?" the lawyer asked with a smile.

"It didn't look romantic," Silas said, "Mary was hitting at him."

"I see," the lawyer added, "but you couldn't be sure he intended to ravish the woman."

"Sir;" Silas said pointedly, "he was pawing at her skirt. Now I've never known a man to pull on a lady's skirt that had good intentions. Have you?" Some members of the jury snickered, and the judge banged his wooden hammer against the desk. The lawyer thanked him, and Silas was free to go.

He went back to the hotel and was sitting in the dining room with Tobias when the entire Locke family came back from the courthouse. They had gone to give Mary moral support as she testified. They sat down with Silas looking completely exhausted.

"How did it go?" Tobias asked.

"He told them I was begging him to kiss me," Mary said, "he said I told him I wanted him. I would never..." she just sat staring at the table.

"The jury didn't believe that any more than we did," Fred said to Mary, putting an arm around her.

"He was found guilty," Susan explained to Silas and Tobias. "The judge said he would have to go to jail for fifteen years." Silas sat back and thought about spending fifteen years locked up. Jake would be over thirty, his life was wasted because he wanted to force himself on someone.

The trial against Burton was just as straightforward. Four men and two women testified they had seen Burton Slade at the cabin the night it was burned down; the jury quickly found him guilty, and he too was sent to prison for fifteen years. Silas thought that at least they would be together.

With the trials finished, they decided to celebrate with dinner at the hotel. They ordered steak, fried chicken, baked potatoes and cake with icing and candied fruit. Silas ate his fill. After they ate and the ladies excused themselves, the men decided to go out for a celebratory drink.

They picked a quiet saloon and sat at a table with their drinks. Cody held his glass up in a toast, "to the final part of the trail!" he exclaimed. They all drank to that.

"I want to thank you men for helping me out," Fred said. "I would likely be dead or wandering looking for new land if you hadn't stopped by."

"Family helps each other," Cody said with a nod. Silas wondered if he had already had too much whiskey with dinner. Silas still didn't like to drink too much but always liked it when Cody did.

"If it ain't Short Hand Trent," came a voice from the bar. Silas turned and saw a man he thought he might recognize. He wasn't very tall, and his dark hair was slicked back. Silas sat there and glared at him.

"Who are you?" Curly asked the man.

"Names Fitch," said the man, "Trent here shot me in the hand a while back, I'd like to return the favor."

Tobais stood and faced the man, "look Fitch, we don't need no trouble, you have your drink, and we'll have ours."

"You going to let your friends do all your talking?" Fitch said, kicking at Silas' chair. Silas stood and faced the man. The man's eyes narrowed, and he reached for his gun. Silas saw him move and palmed his colt as fast as he had been practicing in secret. He fired before the man had his gun halfway up. Fitch gasped and fell back against the bar as his chest opened up.

Silas expected he would never get rid of the name Short Hand Trent now.

Read the first chapter of the next book in the series
Return to the Lazy K

Silas Trent looked across the plain towards home. He was finally home. It had been a year since he left home to avenge his father and get back the cattle that had been stolen. He had brought them home to the Lazy K ranch. With him were his closest friends, Cody, Tobias, Curly and Zeke. They had overcome the great challenges of the trail to get here.

"That's it boys!" he yelled, pointing to the small house sitting close to the base of a hill. It was a rock house that his father had built, it had a low roof and a porch that ran along the front of it. There were two chairs on the porch facing the field where the cattle would sometimes graze. Silas led them down to a gate into the fenced field that was home for his cattle. The cowboys let out a loud whoop as they finished the long drive.

Martha Trent had been sitting at the kitchen table mending clothes, when she heard the ruckus of the cattle returning and rushed to the door to see what all the commotion was. She was surprised to see cows in the fields that had been laid empty for over a year. She saw a man leading them in, long blond hair and square jaw. It looked like her boy Silas, but somehow different. She went to the door to investigate.

Silas was off his horse and was walking to the house. He felt excitement and a sense of dread. He had left without his mother's permission; would she forgive him? While he had not managed to bring the whole herd his father had built, he had enough to start again. Maybe that would help her understand why he had to do what he did. The door to the house opened and his mother stepped out.

Mother and son just stood there for a minute. Silas took in the sight of the woman that raised him, her auburn hair, tied in a bun on the top of her head, her hazel eyes shining with tears. She dropped the mending in her hands and rushed out to her prodigal son and threw her arms around him. He was taller than her four foot eleven, he had been shorter than her when he left. He had grown up while away, his face looked so much older, and his blue eyes showed a maturity she had never seen in him before.

"My Silas!" she exclaimed. "My boy!" She broke down crying.

"I'm home Ma," Silas said, kissing the top of her head. "I did it, I got Pa's cattle back." Silas let go of his mother and escorted her over to the fence to look at the cows who were exploring the space. She looked at him and smiled. Silas called his friends over and introduced them to his Ma. When he mentioned Cody Locke's name his Ma stopped him.

"You Jane Locke's boy?" she asked.

"Yes Ma'am," said Cody.

"Your mother wrote to me a few times," she said, "kept me up with all that was going on. Let me know Silas was safe. When you see her, please thank her for me."

"That would be my pleasure," Silas said with a smile. There was an awkward silence now as nobody really knew what to say. Martha stood and looked at her son; he was almost a man. His fifteenth birthday had passed when he was gone, it had been a hard day. Even though she had received letters saying Silas was alive and well, she was constantly worried. She had already lost a husband and one boy, losing Silas, would have destroyed her.

Silas broke the silence by suggesting that his friends go to the small bunkhouse and get settled. The "bunkhouse" was really just a room off a small storehouse that sat a few yards from the house. It too was stone construction and had a tack room and space for some grain sacks. To one side was a small room with four bunks. When they entered the room, it looked like it hadn't been touched since Silas' Pa was alive. Everything was covered with dust and cobwebs.

"I haven't had the heart to touch anything since Samuel passed," Martha said as she looked around the room. Silas put an arm around his Ma.

"We'll clean," Zeke said looking around. Zeke was a large man with leathery skin and no hair on his head. He was a bit slow in talking but a good cattleman and had saved Silas' life a number of times. He had decided that since Silas had lost his father at a young age, he needed someone to look after him. Silas was often glad he did.

"He's right ma'am," Cody said with a big smile. Cody had this smile that made you think everything was going to be alright, even when common sense said it wasn't. "Now you two have some catching up to do and we will take care of ourselves." Cody shooed them out of the bunkhouse.

Silas walked the familiar path from the bunkhouse to the main house, memories of times with his father rushing back. Walking across the threshold into the house was like he never left. The main area of the house was a big square room with a fireplace along the wall opposite the door, there were two doors on the left that went into the bedrooms. On the right was the door to the kitchen. Martha told Silas to sit at the table and out of habit he sat in the same chair he had sat in for every meal since he was small. Martha smiled and sat in her seat. She put her hands on his and smiled.

"I'm glad you're home," she said, "I bet you have so many stories to tell."

"Ma," Silas looked at her, "I'm sorry about sneaking off like I did." Martha gave his hand and squeezed.

"I was very upset with you for a long time," Martha said, "Jed helped me realize you were just doing what your Pa would have you do." Silas breathed a sigh of relief, and then his mind triggered on something.

"Who's Jed?" he asked.

"Jed Boone," Martha said like that should clear everything up. She could see by his expression that it didn't, so she continued, "he owns the Flying B Ranch. He brought you to me when you were hurt." Silas realized then who she meant. Of course, he remembered the name now. He also remembered his Pa saying that Boone was a no-good tinhorn that would have failed as a rancher if he didn't hire a good foreman. His foreman was Walt Pollard, who had worked a few drives for Silas' Pa before Boone showed up.

"He's been around?" Silas asked.

"He's been a real help," Martha said, "he offered to help after you left." Silas did not like the sound of this but decided it was probably a good thing that someone came to help. He barely knew the man, so maybe it was a good thing.

"I'm glad to hear it," Silas said with a slight smile.

"Now tell me all about your journey," Martha said. Silas talked late into the night about his time in Colorado with the Locke family. Finding the man that had killed his Pa and his brother and watching him die in a gunfight. He told her about his trip home, a few of the dangers he faced, and helping a family save their own ranch. He didn't tell her as much about the gunfights or the men he had to kill. Now, sitting in his family home, it all seemed like a dream.

It was late so Silas gave his Ma one last hug before going into his room. His Ma had been keeping this room clean. He looked over at the second bed, Matt's bed. He hadn't thought much about the brother he had lost, but now as he stared at his bed, he realized how much he missed having his older brother around.

www.ingramcontent.com/pod-product-compliance
Lightning Source LLC
Chambersburg PA
CBHW021333060726
47591CB00006B/2003